Olivia
Flies High

"Liv!" cried Tom. Startled, and about to launch herself into space, Olivia lost her grip. The trapeze juddered and gave a violent twist, and she slipped. She clutched for the rope but it was beyond her grasp and she fell towards the ground like a wounded bird shot down by a hunter. She hit the mats with a terrible, final thud...

Have you read the first book in the series?

Olivia's First Term

"Hugely enjoyable"
The Stage

Look out for:

Olivia and the Movie Stars
Olivia's Enchanted Summer

Olivia
Flies High

LYN GARDNER

nosy
crow

For Ellie and Izzy

First published in the UK in 2011 by Nosy Crow Ltd
The Crow's Nest, 11 The Chandlery
50 Westminster Bridge Road
London, SE1 7QY, UK

Nosy Crow and associated logos are trademarks and/or registered
trademarks of Nosy Crow Ltd

A CIP catalogue record for this book will be available from the
British Library

Printed and bound in the UK by Clays Ltd, St. Ives Plc
Typeset by Tiger Media Ltd, Bishops Stortford, Hertfordshire

Papers used by Nosy Crow are made from wood grown in
sustainable forests.

ISBN: 978 0 85763 025 4

www.nosycrow.com

Chapter One

Olivia Marvell jumped lightly on to the low wall outside the stage door of the Duke's Theatre, flipped forwards on to her hands, and walked the entire length of the wall upside down as if it was the most natural thing to do in the world. Her little sister, Eel, and her friend, Aeysha, clapped enthusiastically. Several passers-by walking down the passage that divided the Duke's from the Royal Vic Theatre next door stopped to applaud, too.

Olivia flashed them a shy grin as she jumped gracefully down, wiped her hands on her jeans and said impatiently, "How much longer? They've been ages. I'm going to explode into a billion pieces if I can't tell them our news soon!"

A gaggle of children emerged from the stage door, adults in tow. Like all the children who had dribbled out in small groups over the last hour, they didn't look too happy. One of the girls was snivelling, and her mother, a glamorous blonde woman with sharp features, said loudly, "Silly man. That director wouldn't know real talent if it bit him on the nose. Never mind, Kelly, we've got bigger fish to fry. You're on the shortlist for that car commercial. It's much better paid."

"But I wanted to be in *The Sound of Music* and sing 'Do-Re-Mi'. . ." whined Kelly, her voice drifting into the distance as they walked down the passageway.

"Not long now; they're down to the last few," said Bert, the stage-door keeper. He'd slipped out from behind his counter just inside the stage door to join Olivia, Eel and Aeysha. Nobody, not even Gus the theatre cat, got into or out of the Duke's without passing by eagle-eyed Bert. He prided himself on knowing everything that was going on and was a fount of delicious gossip.

"So do you think that Tom and Georgia will be cast in *The Sound of Music*?" asked Eel, doing the little wriggle that had given her her nickname.

Bert shrugged. "The longer they're kept back, the better it looks for them. But there's another group of kids coming back for a final audition this afternoon, so nothing's certain. The director, Jon James, and the casting director may not finally make up their minds for days. And of course Chuck Daniels'll be trying to stick his oar in."

"Who's Chuck Daniels?" asked Aeysha.

"He's important; he's the producer. He raised the money to stage the show. Anyway, they'll want to decide which kids they think will work well together in which teams. I doubt anyone will be told today, although I have known it happen."

"Teams? It makes it sound as if they're going to play netball," said Eel, wrinkling her nose.

"No," explained Bert with a smile. "If you don't count Liesl, as that's a main role, there are six Von Trapp children. But they'll cast eighteen children in the roles and split them into three teams. Each team rehearses and performs together and the three teams share the eight performances a week between them. That way nobody gets too tired. But it does mean auditioning a lot of children."

"I'd hate to have to do an audition," said Olivia vehemently, pushing back her curtain of dark hair. "If I had to choose between going to an audition and going to the dentist for a filling, I'd choose the dentist."

"You're just weird, Livy," said Eel, pirouetting very fast across the passageway and causing a man in a pinstripe suit to glare at her. She came to a stop with her chestnut curls still dancing and said, "Oh, I wish, I really, *really* wish that I was auditioning," so dramatically that Olivia, Aeysha and Bert smiled at her heartfelt passion.

"Why aren't you?" asked Bert. "You'd make a cute Gretl."

"I would, wouldn't I; I'm small enough," said Eel with a smile and a twirl. "But Granny Alicia wouldn't let me. She said it would be bad for my technique, and that I hadn't been at the Swan long enough to take part in a professional show. She said that I need to learn to dance properly before I can do auditions. Livy and I have only been Swans for a term. Before that we

4

were with our dad in a travelling circus." She did a perfect cartwheel as if to demonstrate the truth of this.

"Your gran's probably right. She and I go way back. Alicia Swan is a legend and the Swan Academy is by far and away the best stage school in the country," said Bert. "I always like having kids from the Swan at the Duke's. The Swans are not just talented. They're well behaved, not like the little monsters from some other schools. They've always got their feet on the ground and their heads screwed on. It's why so many of them do well."

"Unlike you, Eel," said Olivia. "You've always got your feet off the ground and your head in the clouds."

Eel stuck her tongue out at her sister affectionately. Gus slunk out of the stage door and wrapped himself around Bert's legs like a furry bandage before leaping on to a window sill. Bert lifted him down.

"That cat won't stop climbing. Last week he got up on the roof and then got completely stuck on that ledge," said Bert. He pointed to the high ledge that ran along the side of the theatre just below the roof. A few rusty flagpoles, long

5

since disused, stuck out from the side of the building just below it. "We had to get the fire brigade out to rescue him. Naughty puss."

"I'm going to burst if I have to wait a minute longer!" said Olivia, pacing up and down. Just then the stage door was flung open and Tom and Georgia came racing out, followed by Abbie Cardew, the Swan Academy's head girl, who had already been cast as Liesl. All three had massive grins on their faces.

"We're in!" shouted Tom and Georgia, hugging Olivia, Aeysha and Eel. Eel's arms and legs got a bit twisted up with Georgia's as she tried to do a little dance of triumph.

"My first West End engagement! My mum will be so proud," said Georgia, her eyes shining so that she looked more like a china doll than ever.

"She will!" said Olivia. "We're *all* mega proud of you."

"They were fabulous! Miss Swan will be delighted with them," said Abbie.

"Who are you each playing?" asked Aeysha.

"We don't know yet," replied Georgia. "They say it's still to be decided. But they must have particular characters in mind. I'd love to play Louisa, but I expect I'll be Brigitta. Louisa is supposed to be older so has to be taller. I bet Tom will get Kurt." Georgia did a little skip of excitement.

"I can't wait for rehearsals to begin," said Tom. "But we don't know everyone who's in our team yet. Apparently there's another final audition this afternoon."

"It's mint," said Georgia. "I was sure I'd blown it after I was sick on stage at the first audition before Christmas."

"The director must've seen it was nerves," said Tom. "I knew you were in with a chance when I heard him say you were really talented, just a bit lacking in confidence."

"Listen," said Olivia. "I've got amazing news too. About *Romeo and Juliet on the High-Wire*." *Romeo and Juliet on the High-Wire*, a wonderfully inventive mix of Shakespeare and circus skills created by Olivia and Tom, had been the Swan entry for the Children's Royal Spectacular last term. Georgia and Aeysha had been part of the team and it had won the competition outright. When they had performed it on Christmas Eve at the London Palladium, its originality had brought the house down. Even Olivia, who saw herself as a circus artist, not an actor, and who had been worried about having to act in front of so many people, had loved the experience. It made her feel tingly inside just to think of it.

"What about it?" asked Georgia.

"Guess!" said Olivia, her eyes sparkling.

"You never will," said Eel with an excited jiggle. "It's the bestest."

"Tell us!" demanded Tom and Georgia together.

"We've been invited to go to New York to perform *Romeo and Juliet* at a special charity benefit on Broadway!" beamed Olivia. Tom gasped and Georgia gave a little scream of excitement. Eel performed another small jig.

"That's amazing! Congratulations," said Abbie. But a sudden look of worry flashed across Tom's freckled face.

"When is this, Liv?"

"End of the month," said Olivia happily. Tom and Georgia looked at each other.

"But, Liv, we won't be able to do it. Rehearsals for *The Sound of Music* start next week."

Olivia stared at them, the colour draining from her face. "They must let you have time off for something as important as this, surely?"

"I don't think it works like that, Olivia," said Abbie slowly. "Tom and Georgia will be part of a team. Going to New York would completely muck up the rehearsal schedule. They're going to have to choose one or the other."

There was a long silence. Olivia looked at the others, willing them to choose *Romeo and Juliet*. A pained expression crossed Tom's face, which had turned almost as red as his hair. Meanwhile Georgia was staring guiltily at her shoes as if they were the most interesting things she'd ever seen.

Finally, after what seemed like hours, Tom spoke. "Liv," he said, not quite meeting her eye. "I'm really, really sorry. I know how much *Romeo and Juliet* means to you. But it's just one night and however exciting it would be to perform in New York, this is our chance to be part of a huge show in the West End. It's what we've been working for since we came to the Swan. I'm so sorry, but we can't not be in *The Sound of Music*."

Olivia felt sick with disappointment. She knew she was being unrealistic to expect Tom and Georgia to give up their opportunity to appear in the West End, but she still felt crushed. A minute ago she had been so full of excitement, so certain that, despite her difficult first term, the decision to stay at the Swan Academy had been the right one, and now she suddenly felt unsure and nervous again, as if realising that her priorities were never going to be the same as everybody else's at the Swan.

Without Tom, who Olivia had been teaching to walk the high-wire and who had demonstrated a natural flair for it, they wouldn't be able to do *Romeo and Juliet*. How silly she had been to think that they would take it as seriously as she did. Nobody at the Swan thought that circus was as important as acting, dancing and singing. She wanted to be generous to her friends, but she felt as deflated as a leaky balloon; tears prickled behind her eyes and her throat itched.

She tried to make herself say, "That's all right. It doesn't really matter," but she couldn't control her disappointment and it made her lash out instead. She turned to Tom. "I thought we were a double act, Tom. I thought you loved the high-wire as much as I do, but clearly I was wrong. It was just a passing fad. Probably just as well you're not that good at it, isn't it? I also thought you were a real friend. But I guess I was wrong about that, too." She turned on her heel and walked stiffly away.

Tom looked stung. "Don't be like that, Liv. Of course I'm your friend," he said. He rushed after her and placed a pleading hand on her arm, but Olivia shook it off.

"Just leave me alone," she said. "Don't you have *rehearsals* to go to? I wouldn't want you to miss out on any *opportunities* or anything." She started to walk faster, even though she longed to stop and run back to them and say she was sorry, she hadn't really meant what she'd said. But she was crying hard now and anyway, what did they care how she felt?

Eel looked stricken and made as if to go after her sister, but Abbie caught her hand and held it firmly. She didn't want Eel running around London with Olivia in that state.

"We've really let her down," said Georgia. "I feel awful."

"You mustn't," said Abbie. "Livy will get over it. Give her time. Sometimes you have to make choices in life and you can't always make the one that will please your friends. If you turned down *The Sound of Music* even though you knew it wasn't the right thing to do, you'd just end up resenting Livy *and* the *Romeo and Juliet* show. I didn't think she'd take it that badly, though." Abbie looked at her watch.

"Come on, I've got to get you back to the academy. We'll just be in time to tell Miss Swan your news before the first-day-of-term assembly."

They waved goodbye to Bert and set off for the school. As they walked along, Eel asked, "Who's going to play Gretl?" No one knew for sure, but they told her about the other children at the audition, and a little girl called Freya who they thought might be Gretl, and another contender called Mia. They were so engrossed that they didn't notice a black four-by-four with tinted windows draw up right outside the Duke's Theatre, or the blonde girl who got out. But she saw them, and a little cat-like smile twitched around the corner of her lips.

"Have you got everything, Katie?" came a voice from inside the car.

"Of course, Dad," replied the girl.

"Good luck, kitten."

The girl winked. "Don't worry, Dad. It's

in the bag." She gave him a wave and then swept through the stage door as if she was a fully fledged star about to meet her adoring audience.

Chapter Two

It was the first day of the spring term at The Swan Academy of Theatre and Dance. On a normal day the pupils did their academic lessons in the morning and after lunch took a series of vocational classes. These included dancing, singing and acting, and all sorts of specialisms such as songwriting, devising, improvisation, classical acting and musical theatre. But the new Swan term always started after lunch, as if to emphasise which were really the most important lessons of the day, and why its pupils were at the Swan and not at an ordinary school.

Many of the pupils hadn't even come in their olive-and-gold school uniform but in the practice clothes they would need for their first lesson. Soon the entire building would ring to the sound of singing, tap-dancing feet and play rehearsals. Some children already had scripts tucked under their arms or were trying to commit lines to memory; others, wearing leg warmers, were using the time to stretch as they waited for the rest of the school to file into the hall.

Olivia was waiting at the far end of the cloakroom for Tom, Georgia and Aeysha. She was sitting behind the lockers right by the door that led directly into the hall, so she couldn't miss them. Several people smiled and said hello as they walked into the hall; others eyed Olivia curiously. Despite the huge success of *Romeo and Juliet*, Olivia was still considered a bit of an outsider by some of the children at the Swan Academy. Eel had immediately been accepted as a Swan because of her sunny personality and obvious talent as a dancer, but Olivia's intensity, her initial resistance to dancing, singing and acting, and her love of circus set her apart from the others. It was made worse by the fact that she and Eel were also Alicia Swan's grand-daughters.

By the time Olivia had got back to school from the Duke's she'd begun to feel really ashamed of her outburst, and angry that she had allowed her disappointment to get the better of her. She wished she could take back the words she had said to Tom. That was impossible, but at least she could apologise for acting like an idiot. She knew her three friends would drop their things off in the cloakroom before going into the hall, and she wanted to catch them on their own to tell them how sorry she was. Olivia's pride made it hard for her to say sorry but she knew that it had to be done and that it couldn't wait. Her friendships with Tom, Georgia and Aeysha were what had kept her at the Swan. Particularly Tom. He'd been the first person to accept her and try to understand her passion for circus. He knew how much walking the high-wire meant to her and, despite what she'd said to him, was very good at it, too.

She heard the door from the foyer open, and some people enter. Then she heard Tom's voice. It was thick with disappointment.

"I really thought Liv would be waiting for us when we got back to school. I can't believe she'd let this destroy our friendship." Olivia grinned and prepared to jump out to surprise them with a smile, when Tom added fiercely,

"She's *so* petty, making such a big thing of it, and making me and Georgia feel awful on what should have been one of the best days of our lives. And she calls *me* a bad friend! It's all over nothing, too, just one night of prancing around on a bit of wire! There's no comparison – a West End show or some rubbishy circus act."

Rubbishy circus act! Olivia was hurt beyond belief. She had thought that Tom of all people understood how she felt about the circus. It was a way of life, and its skills were art forms. To hear someone she had trusted so deeply talk about it like that was crushing; it was like being stamped on.

Olivia had thought Tom really cared about the high-wire when he'd just been laughing at her all along. She felt tears gnawing behind her eyes and a gutting sadness, and the thought of her so-called friends finding her there and knowing she had heard what Tom had said was too humiliating. She opened the door into the hall and slipped into the throng like a ghost.

So she didn't hear Georgia say, "Come on, Tom, that's nonsense. We all know you're almost as crazy about circus as Livy. You don't mean that."

Tom looked shamefaced. "No, Georgia, of course I don't. I'm just angry with Liv. It's so hard to make her believe how much I like her. It's as if she wants me to prove myself all the time, to demonstrate that I'm worthy to be her friend."

"I think it's the other way round," said Aeysha, with a flash of the insight for which she was known. "It's more that she doesn't feel worthy to be your friend, that she's surprised you like her so much. Despite the success of *Romeo and Juliet*, she still feels like a fish out of water here at the Swan. As if she doesn't quite belong."

Tom sighed. "Maybe. All I know is that Liv Marvell doesn't make it easy to be her friend. But I miss her loads already, so I guess I'll have to be the one to make the first move."

Alicia Swan, who had founded the school after her own hugely successful stage career had been halted by crippling arthritis, gazed down at her pupils. She loved their energy and their hard-working, sunny optimism. Alicia chose her pupils very carefully, after a long and demanding audition process; talent was necessary but attitude counted for a great deal, too. During her own career she had seen too many bright stars shine brightly then crash and burn, and she wanted Swan pupils to leave the school not just with a first-class training, but also equipped with the attitude and temperament to sustain long and successful careers.

Alicia knew that lots of children had some talent; many wanted to be famous. But talent and desire were not sufficient. They also needed some luck, or what Alicia often called "a little patch of sunlight", and the determination to keep on practising and getting better however many knocks and rejections they received along the way. What they didn't need was arrogance and the misplaced belief that the Swan Academy needed them more than they needed the Swan. The previous term she'd regretfully had to ask Katie Wilkes-Cox to leave after she had admitted trying to frame Olivia for theft. Alicia still wondered whether she had done the right thing. If Katie, a talented student cursed with pushy parents, had been allowed to stay on, perhaps she might eventually have stopped chasing easy fame and put in some hard work.

Alicia briefly wondered where Katie was

now before her eye fell on her granddaughters. Eel was smiling as usual, but Olivia was standing apart from her class looking like someone who'd just got home to discover the ceiling had fallen in. Alicia sighed. She loved both her grandchildren dearly, and was happy to give them a home. But she wasn't always finding being a grandmother easy.

Little Eel was no problem. She was happy just as long as she could dance and perform; she was a natural. But Olivia was a much more complex child, whose love of circus and aptitude for high-wire walking had initially put her on a collision course with her grandmother. The collision had been averted with the success of *Romeo and Juliet on the High-Wire*, which had made Alicia appreciate the creative possibilities of the circus, but her relationship with Olivia was not straightforward.

Alicia's daughter, Toni, who had died in a plane crash when Eel was still a baby, had been a great actress and Alicia was certain that Olivia had inherited Toni's talent. Olivia thought of herself as a circus artist though, never an actor. Alicia hoped that eventually she'd be able to open Olivia's eyes to her own talent.

Abbie had told Alicia what had occurred outside the theatre that morning. Alicia guessed that Olivia's disappointment at not being able to go to New York had something to do with the fact that it might have been a chance to see her dad. Jack Marvell, otherwise known as the Great Marvello, was a daredevil high-wire artist who was attempting to walk across Snake Canyon in Idaho while a film company made a documentary about him. Jack and Olivia adored each other; Alicia thought they were both like wild swooping birds who would never be entirely tamed.

She sighed. She hoped that some news she was going to announce would put a smile back on Olivia's face, and cleared her throat. The hall fell silent immediately.

"Good afternoon, everyone, and welcome back. I'm delighted to see you all and I hope that you're ready for a term of serious hard work and serious fun. We've had a thrilling Christmas holidays and my congratulations to all of you who took part in *Romeo and Juliet on the High-Wire*, which was such an enormous success. I know that some of you have probably heard the show has been invited to New York,

21

but sadly that won't be possible. . ." She paused to allow the groans in the room to subside. "But the reason for that is one of the show's leading performers, Tom McCavity, has been cast in *The Sound of Music* along with another member of the *Romeo and Juliet* team, Georgia Jones! I know you'll join me in wishing them lots of luck." There was clapping and stamping of feet.

Alicia continued. "Of course, they're not our only successes. Aeysha Aziz has a major role in the new Tracy Beaker movie and will be off on an eight-week shoot from the middle of the month. Many congratulations to Aeysha."

Olivia joined in the applause mechanically, but she felt bereft. Perhaps it didn't really matter that she had fallen out with her three best friends seeing as they would all be busy during the coming term anyway. One of her reasons for staying at the Swan was because of all the fun they had together. But it was as if they had already moved on since last term and would be off doing exciting things, while she was stuck at school without them. She suddenly felt as lonely and as nervous as she'd felt on her very first day at the Swan last September.

"For those of you who weren't successful at

the *Sound of Music* auditions, there will be plenty of other opportunities to try for professional work this term. Please keep an eye on the notice board, where auditions will be posted, and then come and see me if you would like to be considered. Do remember, though, that only those doing well in their academic studies can be put forward for professional engagements."

Alicia paused.

"Now I have some really exciting news for you all! The success of *Romeo and Juliet on the High-Wire* has made me realize that the Swan's range of training needs to expand. The theatre world is changing and we must change with it. So I'm delighted to announce that, as of this term, circus skills will be part of the curriculum." There were gasps from the auditorium, and several heads turned to look at Olivia, who blushed scarlet. Her grandmother continued, "So I'd like you all to give a warm welcome to our newest member of staff: Pablo Catalano."

A cheer went up, although only Olivia and Eel were familiar with the name. They looked at each other in surprise and then broke out into grins. Pablo, a rather dashing man with thick curly hair and fiery eyes, was their dad's agent and a very fine circus teacher; it was a coup for the Swan to get him.

He winked at Olivia from the stage. She immediately felt the connection between him and her dad and smiled shyly back. Jack had only left for the US the day after Boxing Day but she already missed him hugely.

Alicia made a few more announcements and then dismissed the school. As the throng began to disperse, Pablo made his way down from the stage and caught Olivia by the arm. "I'm going to need you, Livy. You must be my left hand."

"Right hand," said Olivia, grinning at Pablo and enjoying his accent, which reminded her of her circus travels.

"I'm going to need loads of help, Livy," said Pablo. "I can't teach all these ducklings on my own. Particularly the high-wire. Alicia tells me what a *magnificent* teacher you were with young Tom." Pablo threw his arms in the air and rolled "magnificent" around on his tongue. He added, "As good as your dad, the Great Marvello."

The praise and mention of Jack made Olivia want to smile, but the reference to Tom made her remember how he had barely hesitated when it had come to choosing between *The Sound of Music* and *Romeo and Juliet*. Tom thought that circus was rubbish. It made her feel bruised and angry all over again.

"Oh," said Olivia loudly. "I doubt you'll find this lot very interested in circus skills. When given the choice, they'll always opt for show business and getting famous. That's all they really care about." Tom, who had been walking by, looked as if Olivia had punched him in the stomach.

Alicia, overhearing this, sighed. She had expected Olivia to be thrilled by Pablo's request for help, and had really hoped that Olivia was settling down at the Swan. After all, she had chosen to stay there. Nobody had forced her. Maybe it hadn't been the right decision after all. Alicia had thought that after the dramas of last term this term would prove less eventful. But it had barely started and already she could see stormy times ahead.

Chapter Three

Olivia jumped off the wire and ran across to the window of the rehearsal room. She peered out wistfully and just caught sight of Georgia, Tom and Aeysha walking away from the Swan towards the park. From the tilt of their heads she could tell they were laughing.

She bit her lip, and for a moment thought about rushing downstairs and catching up with them. She'd been invited. Georgia had made a point of looking for Olivia and asking her to go with them, but Olivia just shook her head and said she was busy, which had made Georgia look really unhappy.

"Please come, Livy," she'd said. "We all miss you. You're being really unfair in making me and Tom feel so bad about doing *The Sound of Music.* Tom's really upset. He doesn't know what he can do to make it better."

Olivia almost melted, but her pride stopped her. She knew that she was being silly and that she was driving her friends away with her own stupid behaviour, but it was almost as if once she'd started, she couldn't stop herself. It was addictive, in the same way that sometimes you couldn't stop eating chocolate even though it was making you feel sick. Part of her wanted to rush up to them and apologise for being so grumpy and resentful, but there was another part of her that wanted to make them suffer because they had made her suffer.

She hated herself for even thinking of it but she had a fantasy of Tom coming to find her, begging her forgiveness and saying of course he'd give up doing *The Sound of Music* if it would make her happy. But she knew that wasn't going to happen, not in a million years, and in fact she was the one who really owed him an apology for being so horrible. But she could still hear him saying "rubbishy circus act" with all that scorn in his voice, and it made her harden her heart against him.

The *Sound of Music* rehearsals began the

next day and it was clear from her friends' faces and their little huddled chats that Tom and Georgia were really excited about it. It made Olivia feel all the more left out. Once they got caught up in the thrill of meeting the rest of their team and the hard work of rehearsals, they wouldn't give her another thought. Aeysha would be off soon, too.

It felt as if everything was going wrong because of what had happened in that split second outside the Duke's Theatre. Even her relationship with the two people she loved most in the world, her dad and Eel, had been tainted by it. Only last night Jack had called from Idaho while Olivia was sitting alone in her bedroom, brooding. By the time it was Olivia's turn to talk to her dad, it was clear that both Alicia and Eel had filled him in on what had been happening, and he wasted no time in telling Olivia that she was behaving badly.

"Honestly, Liv, sweetheart. Be reasonable," he'd said. "I know it's disappointing. But if it were the other way round and you got a long-term gig in the circus, you wouldn't give it up to do a one-night performance somewhere else, would you?"

In her heart, Olivia knew that he was right, but she felt mortified that Alicia and Eel had been discussing her with Jack. If only he was here, she could have talked the whole thing through with him. But he was thousands of miles away, so far away he might just as well have been on the moon, and that thought made her feel so lonely that she could barely speak. It felt as if someone had stuffed a brick down her throat.

If Jack had been able to see her, he would have realised this, but instead he mistook her terse replies and silence for sulkiness. The conversation had ended with Jack saying, "You really need to get over yourself, Liv," and Olivia slamming the phone down on him. She felt completely abandoned; even her dad was against her!

Her shoulders sagged. She had been so bound up in herself that she hadn't even asked him how the preparations were going for his walk across Snake Canyon. It was a very dangerous stunt, performed deep in the heart of a wilderness. The team was using a light aircraft to cover the terrain and would also be filming the stunt from the air as the centrepiece of the documentary. Olivia had wanted to ask him what it was like flying in such a tiny plane. She felt so miserable and furious with herself that later she had turned her anger on Eel.

"You're a horrid little sneak to talk to Dad about me," she railed. "You don't even know anything about it."

"Yes, I do! I was there when you stormed off, remember," said Eel mutinously. "I felt sorry for you, Livy. So did the others; everyone knows how much *Romeo and Juliet* means to you. I'm disappointed too. I wanted to go up the Empire State Building. But *you're* the one not talking to Aeysha, Tom and Georgia. They want to make up. They're all really upset that you've got the hump. Particularly Tom."

"Have you been talking to my friends about me behind my back?" demanded Olivia furiously.

"Well, somebody has to talk to them if you won't," said Eel reasonably, doing the little hop she did when she was nervous. Olivia was making her really edgy. Her sister had a short temper and often suddenly exploded with anger, but she was usually quick to say sorry. Eel had never known her to hold a grudge like this before.

"Well, I bet they didn't tell you that Tom said *Romeo and Juliet* is just a rubbishy circus act, did they?"

Eel looked shocked. "Oh, Livy, there must be some mistake. I'm sure he doesn't believe that. Tom loves the tightrope almost as much as you do."

"Look, Eel, it's none of your business, so just buzz off. Stay away from them and stay away from me, too. You'll just make everything worse with your babyish meddling."

Eel flinched. Olivia had never spoken to her so harshly before. She ran back into the living room where Alicia was on the phone to someone in Hollywood.

Remembering that conversation now, Olivia slumped against the wall. She'd been unforgivably horrible to her beloved little sister. The list of people she needed to apologise to just kept getting longer and longer. She muttered furiously to herself: "You're a complete idiot, Olivia Marvell, and your own worst enemy."

"Yes, and you're cutting off your toes to spite your feet."

Olivia spun around. It was Pablo.

"You shouldn't listen in when people

are talking to themselves, it's rude," she said, embarrassed. "And it's nose and face, not toes and feet."

Pablo shrugged, his eyes sparkling. "It's the same thing," he said. "The only person who feels the pain is you." He pretended to stab himself through the heart and rolled his eyes dramatically. "How's the wire-walking coming along?" he asked. "Have you been practising the new routine you and Jack were working on before he left?"

Olivia sighed. "It's not the same without Tom. It was fun being a double act."

"There's no reason why the two of you shouldn't be a double act again. You must make up with him. He's not going to be in *The Sound of Music* for ever, and once the rehearsals are over he'll be able to practise with you again."

"He won't want to," said Olivia, gloomily.

"He won't if you keep cutting off the toes," said Pablo seriously, pushing back his dark curls. "Listen, Miss Alicia sent me to get you. She's got a surprise for you."

"Nice or nasty?" asked Olivia nervously.

"Magnificent, of course!" grinned Pablo. "Not that Miss Grumpy deserves a surprise.

But come and see. We must not keep Miss Alicia waiting. She is very scary if you do that."

"How do you know?"

"I was a day late for my interview. I got my Wednesdays mixed up with my Thursdays. I felt like a very naughty boy." Pablo grinned. "But I still got the job, and I like the Duck Academy and all the little ducklings very much."

Olivia smiled. She knew Pablo was trying to cheer her up and she felt grateful.

Alicia was waiting for them just outside the school hall. She didn't look at all impatient. In fact, she looked unusually nervous, but she smiled when she saw Olivia.

"This isn't my idea, Olivia," she said. "It's your dad's. He rang me late last night. I wasn't at all sure about it. But I discussed it with Pablo – he's the expert after all – and he was all for it."

"Dad rang you?" cried Olivia. "Last night?"

Alicia nodded.

Olivia suddenly felt a lightening of her heart. He couldn't have turned against her completely then! "What is it?" she asked eagerly.

Alicia opened the door and the others

followed her through. Hanging from the high rafters, fully rigged, was a swinging trapeze.

Olivia gasped. "For me?"

Alicia nodded. "And Pablo, and maybe some of the others in the school if any of them show any real aptitude." She gave a little shudder. "Although I'm not sure I really want them to. All this circus business seems so risky. Nobody ever got hurt doing a *plié*."

"Miss Alicia, I've explained before it is not about risk, it is about *managing* risk. I will look after your little ducklings; I will not let them fall," said Pablo soothingly.

He turned to Olivia. "Jack said that you'd done much static and swinging trapeze work the summer before last when you were all in Italy, and he tells me that you are a girl who can fly. He thought a break from the high-wire might do you good, and the trapeze is something that you and I can do together. You know it's my speciality, along with the *castell*."

Olivia nodded enthusiastically. She had gone with Eel, Tom, Georgia and Aeysha to see Pablo make a guest appearance on the swinging trapeze with the Cirque du Soleil at the Albert Hall on New Year's Day, which had been thrilling.

Jack had also told her that Pablo was famous for creating *castells*, the human towers or castles that hailed from the Catalan region of his native Spain. It was a skill that required great strength, agility and balance from the participants, who had to create a strong base of people at the bottom before others clambered up them like monkeys to create wedding-cake-style human tiers that rose high into the air. While travelling with the circus in Spain, Olivia had seen human towers eight or nine tiers tall, as high as a house, often with a tiny child as young as five perched on the very top. They required massive skill and balance and everybody had to work as a team to be successful.

"I'm going to start the ducklings off by learning how to create *castells*, and maybe do some more high-wire walking as you've already got them going. . ."

But Olivia wasn't really listening. She was looking at the trapeze with shining eyes as if she was already imagining swooping through the air like a bird. "When can we start the trapeze?" she asked impatiently.

"Right now," said Pablo. "But first you've

got to promise me and your grandmother two things, Livy."

"What?"

Alicia looked grave. "One, you'll stop being silly and make it up with Tom and your other friends. Friendship is much too important to fool around with, Olivia. Secondly, and this is really serious, that you'll *never* practise the trapeze without Pablo being present."

Pablo nodded. "The trapeze is very different from the wire," he said. "You're very experienced on that, and if you do slip in the rehearsal room, it's not so far to fall. You do not break the head or the arms or the neck. But with the trapeze? *Madre mia!* You could do yourself a big injury if you came off the trapeze. *Terminado.*" He made a gesture as if cutting his throat. Alicia gave another little shudder.

"I promise," said Olivia.

"Right, partner," said Pablo. "Let's see what you can do."

Alicia felt delighted by the smile on Olivia's face. She'd hated to see her so unhappy. She was watching her granddaughter shimmy up the rope when her mobile rang. It was another call from Hollywood. She hurried away to take it.

36

Chapter Four

The next morning, Olivia was waiting just inside the glass doors of the Swan, hopping from one foot to another. She had two good luck cards in her hands that she had stayed up late making while Eel had gone to see Matthew Bourne's *Nutcracker!* at Sadler's Wells with one of her friends. One was for Tom and the other was for Georgia.

She also had a little "Sorry" card stuffed inside her pocket that she'd made for Eel and which she had wanted to give to her at breakfast but, inspired by *Nutcracker!*, Eel had rushed off early for an extra ballet class.

Olivia knew that the children's rehearsals for *The Sound of Music* started that afternoon and, having taken everyone's words to heart, she wanted to make it up with her friends before they were swept up in the hard work of preparing for the show. The cards were a peace offering and she had been really creative with them.

She looked impatiently out of the glass doors as the bell rang for morning lessons. Where on earth were they? Then she saw Aeysha hotfoot it up the road and take the steps outside the school two at a time, laden down with her saxophone and a bag full of practice clothes.

"Hi, Livy, what's up?" Aeysha asked a little hesitantly. She felt wary of Olivia in case she snapped at her.

"I'm waiting for Tom and Georgia," said Olivia. "Do you know where they are?"

Aeysha saw the cards in Olivia's hands and guessed what they were. "Oh, Livy, you've missed them," she said. "They're not coming to lessons this morning. They've got a costume fitting before rehearsals start this afternoon. They only heard about it late yesterday afternoon when we were in the park. I met them for breakfast. They were both so excited. If only you'd come to the park, you'd have known about meeting up for breakfast today and could have joined us."

"Oh," said Olivia in a small voice.

"You can give them the cards tomorrow."

"It won't be the same," said Olivia sadly. "I wanted Tom and Georgia to know how sorry I am about being mean before they started rehearsals."

"Why don't you call Tom?" suggested Aeysha.

"I don't have a phone, remember. Gran won't let me have one until my birthday in May. She thinks you have to be thirteen to have a mobile phone, unless you've got a good reason like you lot do, travelling to and from school each day on your own. It's so stupid, and makes me feel like a freak. I'm the only person in the year without one."

"You can use mine," said Aeysha kindly. Olivia was smiling at her gratefully when they heard a voice behind them.

"Come along, girls, you shouldn't be chatting here, you should be in double maths," said Miss Hanbury, the voice teacher, who had spotted them in the hallway. "Quick, or I'll have to give you both a misconduct." Olivia and Aeysha hurried off to the classroom.

"You can borrow it at lunchtime," said Aeysha, and she reached out for Olivia's hand and squeezed it. "It's good to have you back, Livy."

But when lunchtime arrived, Olivia got cold feet about ringing Tom. What if he didn't answer and she just had to leave a message? What would she say? Or even worse, what if he answered and put the phone down when he realised it was her and not Aeysha? She wouldn't blame him. She had been so unreasonable over the whole *Sound of Music* thing, she thought that by now he might not want to make up with her at all.

"Thanks for the offer of the phone, Aeysha," she said, "but I've changed my mind; I'll see them tomorrow. Some things are easier said face to face."

Leaving Aeysha staring after her, she rushed off to find Pablo. She'd promised to help run the first lunchtime *castell* session. There was a big turn-out of children, including William Todd and Libby Oakham from Olivia's class who had already proved themselves keen tightrope-walkers. Olivia was quite surprised to see Katie Wilkes-Cox's former friend Kylie Morris, who

40

had previously shown a disdain for anything to do with the circus. She guessed that Kylie might have come to get a closer look at Pablo, whose long curls made him look like the hero from a nineteenth-century romantic novel. Judging by their giggles, some of the older girls were there for the same reason.

But it was the presence of Kasha Kasparian and his Year Eleven friends, Ryan O'Connor and Jazz Quarshie, that was creating a buzz. Kasha, a talented singer who had just signed a solo recording contract, didn't turn up for any non-compulsory class unless it was cool to be seen doing so. Word that he was at Pablo's lesson spread in a twinkling and there was a late rush to join the class that had been given the Kasha stamp of approval.

"Now you are all here we shall make our very first *castell*," said Pablo. "This will make me very proud because in Catalonia, where I come from, we make the human castles very often. They can be very tall, as high as a big house. Even very tiny children like Emmy here," he pointed to a ringletted cherub who was a great friend of Eel's in Year Three, "climb to the very top of these towers without fear because they know that everyone at the base will be strong and keep them safe. Olivia, please show the video."

Olivia had wangled two laptops from the office which she had connected to YouTube. The children split into two groups to gather around the computers. Olivia pressed play and a video of a group of *castellers* building a tower began. The largest and strongest people moved into position, their legs braced and their arms tight around each other to create a sturdy foundation. As soon as the base was in place, more people scrambled up over their friends' bodies to create the next tier. In the space of a few seconds the structure seamlessly grew taller and taller; it was like watching the speeded-up film of a tree growing, although in this case the trunk was made entirely of people. When they had gone as high as they could, the tower was slickly dismantled in what seemed like a second.

Everyone clapped when the brief video came to an end.

"It's really cool; it's like a human wedding cake," said Kasha.

Pablo nodded.

"I want to go right to the very top," said Emmy.

"Then we must start immediately," grinned Pablo, pleased by their enthusiasm. He looked around and pointed at the older boys and some of the girls.

"You too, duckling," he said to Kylie Morris. "I need the stout people to make the *pinya*, which is what we call the base in my country."

"Oh!" shrieked Kylie. "He thinks I'm fat!"

Kasha raised his eyes heavenwards and shook his head. "Don't be dumb, Kylie. He means strong, not fat."

Kylie, who didn't know whether to be outraged that Kasha had called her dumb or delighted that he even knew her name, was mollified and joined the others who stood barefoot, shoulder to shoulder, their arms wrapped around each other. Pablo selected another group of children.

"Now," he said, "you must slither like eels up their backs and form another layer of the wedding cake." With much laughing and the occasional "ouch" as a foot was placed on a head rather than a shoulder, they created another layer. Pablo was impressed: the Swans' years of training in dance had made them both strong and agile, essential qualities needed to create a *castell*.

"We will try one more level," said Pablo. "The littlest ducklings must climb now like the naughty little monkeys they are."

Emmy and her friends giggled as they climbed over the shoulders of the other Swans. The base began to sway with the added weight. Kasha said something rude under his breath. The second tier began to wobble dangerously and suddenly the whole thing collapsed like a deflating soufflé. Everyone ended up on the rubber mats in a great big laughing heap just as Alicia walked into the hall.

Pablo shot Olivia a worried look. He suspected that Alicia might not be too happy to see some of her best dancers falling into a heap of twisted arms and legs, but she was so preoccupied that she hardly noticed the collapsing *castell*.

"Ah, Olivia, there you are. Could you come up to the flat just as soon as you're finished here, please? I need to talk to you urgently."

Olivia was puzzled. She couldn't think of

anything she'd done that merited her returning to the flat during the day. Normally if Alicia wanted to talk to pupils, she did it in her office, and during the school day she treated Olivia and Eel like pupils, not grandchildren. Olivia could see the others eyeing her curiously. She hated it when the other Swans were reminded that she was Alicia's granddaughter.

"I'll be up in just a tick," she said.

Alicia nodded briskly and swept away. Nobody would know from her graceful movements how badly her arthritis affected her.

Everyone started to put away the mats. "That was buff. Can we try again tomorrow?" said William.

"If you'd like to," said Pablo, delighted by the response.

"Yes," said Kasha. "We would. We want to make the tallest human castle in the world."

Pablo grinned, and went to help Olivia put the last of the mats away. "I'm free after school tonight if you want to do some more trapeze?" he said.

"Yes, please," said Olivia. "I love it," she added shyly. "It makes me feel so free and dreamy. It must be how birds feel when they are soaring in the sky."

Pablo smiled. It was exactly how it made him feel too. "Go, Livy. You must not keep Miss Alicia waiting."

Olivia climbed up the stairs to the flat. She pushed open the door and was surprised to see two suitcases in the hall. She wondered whether Alicia had a guest to stay. But when she walked into the living room, Alicia was wearing a coat, and her handbag and passport were sitting on the table. Alicia was going somewhere. During term-time. Olivia knew it must be very important for her to leave her beloved Swans. Her heart started thumping and she felt a sudden terror.

"It's Dad, isn't it? Something's happened to Dad!"

Alicia looked perplexed. "Jack?" Then a look of understanding passed across her face. "No, Olivia darling, nothing terrible like that," she said, walking across the room and putting her arms around Olivia. "How silly of me to frighten you. You always think the worst. Jack's fine. I spoke to him only an hour ago."

"Then where are you going?" asked Olivia.

"To Hollywood!"

Olivia's eyes widened. "Are you going to make a movie?"

"Yes," said Alicia. "With Peter Jackson, who made *The Lord of the Rings*."

Olivia swallowed. "That took three years," she said and hugged Alicia fiercely. Alicia was very touched; spontaneous demonstrations of affection from her eldest granddaughter were few and far between.

"I'll only be gone for three weeks," said Alicia. "Mine is just a tiny part. My real job will be to try and coax a good performance out of the Wood twins. They're the stars, but it seems that Wood is a very good name for them."

Even Olivia had heard of Cosmo and Cosima Wood. They were the youngest members of a great American acting dynasty and had been appearing on TV since they were a few days old. They launched their own fashion range when they were six and for the last few years had starred in their own TV show that was shown all over the world. They were the same age as Olivia but were already said to be worth millions.

"Livy, this has all happened so quickly I haven't had a chance to discuss it with you and Eel. I only heard about the possibility a few days ago and it was just this morning that they called to say that if I was going to come, it had to be today. But if you really don't want me to go, then of course I'll stay."

Olivia looked at her grandmother's face. She knew that the chance to act again meant a great deal to Alicia. "Of course I think you should do it!" she said. "But how will the Swan run without you?"

"Like clockwork," said Alicia, smiling broadly. "Sebastian Shaw will be in charge and all the rest of the staff will pull together. I'm doing this for the school too, not just for me. They are paying me very handsomely indeed. So well that I'll finally have enough to secure a mortgage on the land next door where that derelict building is. It means the Swan will be able to expand."

"That's brilliant!" A sudden thought struck Olivia. "What about Eel and me while you're away? Where will we live?"

"I discussed it with Jack. Eel is sorted. I spoke to her while you were helping Pablo. She's going to go and stay with Emmy Lovedale's family around the corner. They all

48

adore her. You've been invited too; they say they'd love to have you, but you could stay here if you would prefer. Miss Hanbury has offered to move in while I'm gone. It will save her the journey each morning." Her grandmother's face grew serious. "You're my main concern, Olivia darling. If you're not happy, I'll cancel the taxi and ring them to say I'm not coming, and we'll say no more about it. I know you've been slow to settle at the Swan and I promised Jack I'd look after you, so if you don't want me to go, I'll quite understand."

But for Olivia, there was no choice. She didn't want any more change in her life, that was true, but she also realised that this was a real opportunity for Alicia and the Swan. If she said no, then she knew that Alicia would feel just as she had felt when *Romeo and Juliet on the High-Wire* had been scuppered.

"Of course you must go!" she said brightly. "I'll stay here with Miss Hanbury."

Alicia gave a huge smile. She reached into her pocket and brought out a mobile phone.

"This is for you, Olivia. I know how much you want one. My number and Jack's number and the Lovedales' number are already stored.

The slightest problem, call me, and don't worry about the cost."

"Don't *you* worry; we'll all be fine," said Olivia, delighted with her phone and feeling rather grown up.

But after waving goodbye to Alicia's taxi, Olivia suddenly felt incredibly alone again. Eel had already said goodbye to Alicia and was back in her afternoon lessons, so Olivia couldn't even talk to her sister. She suddenly realised that she still had the crushed card for Eel in her pocket, along with the ones for Tom and Georgia. If only she hadn't fallen out with her friends, she might have been staying at one of their houses, rather than on her own with Miss Hanbury in the flat.

The urge to try to speak to Tom was suddenly huge. She felt as if she couldn't wait another moment to apologise. She knew Tom's number because he was always laughing at the word it spelled out if you turned his phone upside down. She looked at her watch. He'd be in rehearsal now. She'd text him. Quickly she composed a text message, entered the number and pressed send. She suddenly felt lighter.

Everything was going to be all right with Tom. They'd be best friends again. She just knew it.

Chapter Five

Tom and Georgia had really enjoyed the costume fitting. They had been met at the costumiers in a back street near Tower Bridge by the assistant director, Josie Cutwell, who'd ticked their names off her list and sorted them into teams. It was a bit chaotic because there were lots of children milling around, several backstage staff from *The Sound of Music* – including the head of costume and her assistant – and the steamstresses who were going to make the four changes of clothes that each child would require.

"Tom McCavity and Georgia Jones, you're in Alps team and you're playing Kurt and Brigitta. Go and join the rest of your team over there and introduce yourselves to the others. You're going to be working closely together over the coming months, so it would be good to get to know each other, and even better if you all got on," said Josie. She turned to one of her colleagues. "*Oliver!* was a complete nightmare because one of the Artful Dodgers fell out with his Oliver and all the other kids took sides. We had to give them all warnings after there was nearly a fight during the curtain call one evening."

Tom and Georgia introduced themselves to the other children. Tom already knew Joshua, the boy playing Friedrich, because they had been in pantomime together, and Georgia discovered that Freya, the girl playing Gretl, was the eight-year-old sister of Liberty, a girl that Aeysha had done a modelling campaign with for a big high-street shop.

"Liberty tried out for *Sound of Music* too. She hoped to get Louisa, but her singing's not strong enough. I was lucky to get Gretl. It's because I'm small for my age, so I can play younger. It's always an advantage at auditions," explained Freya.

"I'm Mia and I'm going to be Marta," said a pale girl with long plaits.

"Who's playing Louisa?" asked Georgia.

The others shrugged and shook their heads.

"Whoever she is, she's very late," said Freya. "It's not very professional, particularly on the first day."

Josie came over to them. "Right then, Alps team, come into the workshop so we can get you all measured up."

"But we haven't got a Louisa yet," piped up Freya.

"Oh, that's all taken care of," said Josie grumpily. She hated always being the one to have to deal with the kids, but that was the lot of the assistant director. "Apparently this morning wasn't convenient for her so she had her fittings at the same time as some of the principals. She's going to meet up with us at the theatre at lunchtime for the first rehearsal." Josie saw their surprised faces. "Don't you get any ideas and expect special treatment like that. Your Louisa isn't just any old child actor; she's the producer's niece. Normal rules don't apply to her, it seems."

After the children had been measured they were taken to the stage door of the Duke's Theatre. Bert greeted them all and showed them where to sign in every day and gave them a few rules: no running in the corridors, no pulling Gus's tail, no chewing gum on the underside of the dressing-room tables, no mucking about with the fire extinguishers.

"I'll know if you do, and then the theatre ghost will get you."

"Does the Duke's have a ghost?" asked Freya, wide-eyed.

"Lots," said Bert. "But they're all friendly. My favourite is the lady in blue. If you see her on the first night, it's a sign of good luck and means the show is going to be a huge success."

Bert took them up to their dressing rooms. The Alps boys had dressing-room seven and the girls were in dressing-room eight. They were delighted to find sandwiches waiting for them – costume fitting was a hungry business. They munched contentedly and listened to more tales of the Duke's colourful history from Bert.

"Until Victorian times these were all one big dressing room and all the leading nineteenth-century actors would have used it. The great clown Joseph Grimaldi did when he was in pantomime here," he explained. "Some actors say that they've seen his ghost peering over their shoulders in the mirror when they're putting on their make-up." Bert pointed to the large mirrors surrounded by bright light bulbs where the children would be able to do their make-up. They all shivered slightly at the thought of the ghostly clown.

Each dressing room had a window that opened out on to the passageway many metres below, but not much light came in because of the Royal Vic Theatre next door. When they had finished eating they left all their stuff in their dressing rooms and were shown the way down the stairs to backstage. They were then taken through into the auditorium where all the teams of children filed into the front rows of stalls.

Tom and Georgia waved excitedly at Abbie, who blew them a kiss before going back to her conversation with the musical director. Abbie had already been in rehearsals with the other principals for two weeks because, although she appeared in the scenes with the children, her role was a leading one. Her name would appear in small letters on the first page of the programme below the title.

Tom and Georgia looked around at the theatre. Backstage, and the stairs and corridors that led to the dressing rooms, was all rather dingy. The paint was even peeling in places. But the auditorium was beautiful. It was, thought Georgia, a bit like finding yourself snuggled inside the red-velvet lining of a very ornate gilt-edged chocolate box. Golden plaster doves hovered over each side of the proscenium arch that framed what happened on stage like a picture. The stage was massive, stretching back like a football pitch.

Georgia couldn't believe that she was going to perform on the very same stage as great actors such as Laurence Olivier, Judi Dench and Toni Swan. She knew that Alicia Swan had appeared on this very stage, too, playing the lead in both *West Side Story* and *My Fair Lady* as well as in some famous plays. She couldn't wait for the moment when she first stepped out to make her West End debut with her mum watching in the audience. She suddenly remembered the story about a famous actress playing Juliet in another theatre who'd just got to the line: "Where is my father and my mother, nurse?" when she heard a cry from the stalls: "Here we are, darling, Row H." Georgia hoped her mum would be better behaved.

The stage manager was overseeing the set

as it was moved into place, and two set dressers were also on stage in discussion with the assistant designer. Suddenly everyone stood aside and fell silent as the director of the show, Jon James, swept on to the stage. He was followed by a small group of people who included the casting director; the producer, Chuck Daniels; assistant director, Josie Cutwell; and the stars of the show. Sam Gibbs, who was playing Captain von Trapp, was a rather dashing older actor who had spent many years with the Royal Shakespeare Company. Cassie Usher, playing Maria, was well known for her role in a TV soap but had asked to be written out of it so she could pursue more stage and film opportunities. She'd been killed off by being pushed off the London Eye, an exit so spectacular that it had been splashed across the front pages of all the tabloid newspapers.

"Oh, look! There's Cassie Usher," said Georgia excitedly. "Isn't she—" But she didn't finish the sentence because her mouth had dropped open. Tom gasped in surprise and made a spluttering noise of disgust. Cassie Usher was chatting animatedly to a tall girl with very blonde straight hair as if the girl was her very best friend in all of the world. Tom and

Georgia recognised the girl immediately. It was Katie Wilkes-Cox, who at the end of last term had been asked to leave the Swan. They stared at each other as a truly horrible thought dawned on them. Now they knew who was going to be Louisa, and both of them wished they didn't. Working with Katie could only be a nightmare. She wasn't the kind of person to forget a grudge.

But Katie didn't even glance in their direction. She just tossed back her blonde hair, sauntered across the stage as if she owned it and disappeared into the wings. A second later she reappeared through the pass door that linked backstage to front of house in the auditorium. She walked confidently down the aisle, sat next to Tom and Georgia, and whispered very sweetly to them, "I've just had lunch with Cassie Usher. She's a sweetheart." She gave a tinkling little laugh. "You two had better close your mouths before you swallow a fly."

"Get me out of here," groaned Tom to Georgia.

"Oh, Ginger, that's not nice," said Katie. "Not nice at all. Anyone would think that you weren't pleased to see me!"

Chapter Six

"Right, unfortunately we'll have to take a break while this is sorted out," said Jon James impatiently. "We've got a technical hitch. Alps team, just pop yourselves in the stalls. You can take the opportunity to start learning your lines. I want you all word perfect by the start of next week."

Tom, Georgia and the others slipped through the pass door and down into the front rows of the auditorium. It felt like passing between two entirely different worlds. A bit like going through the wardrobe into Narnia, thought Tom.

Lakes and Meadows teams had gone to the rehearsal room in Clapham, where they were learning a dance. But Alps team, scripts in hand, had remained at the theatre to start blocking the von Trapp children's first meeting with Maria.

Blocking was when all the actors' positions and movements on the stage were plotted, and it ensured that everybody knew exactly where they should be standing and moving during the scene so that nobody bumped into anybody else and everyone could be seen from the auditorium.

Jon James and Josie were moving around different parts of the auditorium to ensure that the view was good from every part of the house. It had been going very well until a problem with the grand sweeping staircase had been discovered. It wasn't properly locked into place and was in danger of moving. For health and safety reasons it had to be dealt with before the rehearsal could continue.

"I've always thought blocking was boring, but knowing it's for a big West End show is making this much more fun," said Georgia, plonking herself down next to Tom.

"Yep, but it's slow work," replied Tom. "What do you think of Katie?" He looked around to check she wasn't near.

Georgia grinned. "She keeps trying to

upstage the rest of us, and Jon James is letting her get away with it. I guess it's because she's the producer's niece."

"She hasn't changed, has she? I thought being asked to leave the Swan might have made her nicer."

"Perhaps she *has* changed for the better, but she's keeping it well hidden," laughed Georgia.

"Well, she couldn't have changed for the worse. That would be impossible." Tom sighed.

"Maybe if we're going to work together we should try to be friends with her?"

"I'd prefer to try and make friends with a piranha," said Tom. "I haven't forgotten what she tried to do to Liv. And she almost succeeded. If things had turned out differently, Katie would still be at the Swan and Liv would have been sent away in disgrace. We should steer clear. She's entirely toxic."

Katie, who had been bending down in the row behind them to tie her shoelace, straightened up. Her cheeks were flaming and she was formulating a crushing put-down, when Tom said, "I wish I knew what to do about Liv. She's so prickly it's like dealing with a hedgehog. She's acting as if she really hates me."

"Olivia's hurt, Tom, because you chose *The Sound of Music* over her and *Romeo and Juliet*. But if we just keep trying to talk to her, eventually she'll crack and realise just how stupid she's being. I know she will."

"I hope so. Liv Marvell's the stubbornest person I've ever met. Still, I'm going to try and have it out with her before school tomorrow. I really want to make it up with her. The longer it goes on with us not talking the harder it gets."

"You'll probably win the Nobel Peace Prize, Tom McCavity," said Georgia.

"As long as I win an Olivier for best supporting actor in a musical at the same time," said Tom. They both laughed, so they didn't notice Katie slipping away. Just then, Jon James called Tom and Joshua back up on stage.

Katie walked into the stage-door area. All the children were supposed to be in the auditorium or on stage but she didn't want to be with the kids. She was above that lot. She might be playing Louisa, but that was only because of her age. She was sure that she could have managed Liesl much better than that insipid Abbie Cardew. During the break she had tried to strike up another conversation with Cassie

Usher, but Cassie, who had been so charming to her over lunch with Katie's uncle, smiled and carried on chatting with Abbie. And Abbie did nothing to include Katie in the conversation. Katie hoped that nobody had noticed Cassie give her the brush-off.

She had watched Jon James working with the boys for a few minutes, but it was dull watching other people perform. Katie only liked it when people were watching her. They were obviously going to be ages. She wandered out to the stage door. She decided she'd go and have a chat with Bert, even though she thought he was old and boring. Everyone said he knew everything that was going on. She might pick up some useful gossip. Information was power, after all. She had already swiped her uncle's list of cast contacts. It made her feel good to have the personal mobile and home numbers of stars such as Sam and Cassie in her phone.

But Bert was just outside the stage door supervising a costume delivery. Katie peered over his counter and tried a couple of drawers. The first two were locked. But one opened. It was the one in which Bert kept the dressing-room keys, a spare for the adult dressing rooms and the spare and the original for all the children's dressing rooms. The keys for the children's dressing rooms had been removed from the doors during last year's production of *Oliver!* after the girl playing Bet had locked the Artful Dodger in and refused to let him out until he apologised for calling her "a talentless, lazy moo".

Katie glanced around. Nobody was about. She picked up both the keys for dressing-rooms seven and eight and slipped them into her pocket, then pushed the other keys a little closer together so the ones she'd taken wouldn't be missed and closed the drawer – just as Bert walked back in. Sensing something suspicious about her behaviour, he said, "Aren't you supposed to be in the theatre?"

Katie shrugged rudely and left, heading up the stairs towards the dressing rooms. Bert sighed. Some of these child actors could be really uppity. He blamed the parents.

Katie looked up and down the corridor to check that nobody was about and slipped into the boys' dressing room. She wasn't looking for anything in particular. She just thought she'd have a poke around. You never knew what you might find. But the boys' dressing room was rather dull, already smelling faintly of sweaty socks and trainers. Joshua was obviously a Chelsea supporter. Someone else had been reading *Stormbreaker*. Katie guessed that was Tom. She yawned. They were all so boring. Just kids.

She was about to leave when she heard the "bleep bleep" of a mobile phone receiving a message. It was coming from the pocket of an olive-green Swan blazer that she knew must belong to Tom. Why not take a look? There were two messages waiting. The first was from Aeysha: *Hope rehearsals brill. Can't wait 2 hear about it.* Katie deleted the message. The second text was from a number that was not stored in Tom's phone. She pressed the read button.

Hi Tom. I've been an idiot. I'm really sorry. U've always been a great friend and stood by me even when every1 was against me, and I've been a rubbish friend 2 u. I hope you have the best time ever doing SOM. I do understand why you chose to do it. I want to make everything all right again. I miss u. Can we meet up before school tomorrow? I'll be waiting for you at 8am. Call me on this number if you can't make it. Gran has given me a mobile. Will explain all. Liv

Katie reread the message. It fitted with the conversation she had overheard between Tom and Georgia. Clearly Olivia Marvell and Tom McCavity had had a big falling-out. Boo hoo. It served them right. If it hadn't been for them and that mousy Georgia Jones, she'd still be at the Swan.

She hated Liver Marvell and she hated Ginger Tom McCavity. At first, when she'd heard that he might be cast in *The Sound of Music*, she had thought that she'd try to use her influence with Uncle Chuck to stop it. But then she decided that it would be more fun if he *did* get the role: she had every intention of making his life a misery in any way that she could. Katie smiled as she deleted the message from Olivia. She was just putting Tom's phone back in his blazer pocket, when she had an idea so brilliant that it made her gasp out loud at her own genius.

She got the cast contact sheet out of her pocket and then slipped out her new state-of-the-art phone with her brand-new number. Her dad had given to her it as a present when she had left the poxy old Swan. What had her dad said?

"Put the past behind you, kitten. Don't look back, and never have any regrets," and he had given her the phone, adding, "A brand-new number for a brand-new life."

Well, it was going to prove very useful now. She pressed the create message button and expertly tapped out the following:

I h8 u Tom McCavity. I never want 2 speak to u ever again. Our friendship is dead. You're cat food as far as I'm concerned and that goes for that smarmy Georgia and sucking up Aeysha 2. Have a horrid life. Olivia.

Then she pressed send. She waited for a moment until she heard the satisfying "bleep bleep" coming from the pocket of Tom's blazer, then she skipped out of the dressing room and back downstairs.

Katie slid back into the auditorium unseen. Nobody had noticed her absence. Jon James was just calling the girls up on stage, and as she took her place she gave him her most dazzling smile.

Chapter Seven

The first day of rehearsals had finished, and Aeysha had rushed over from the Swan to meet Tom and Georgia at the little café round the corner from the theatre. She had looked for Olivia to see if she wanted to come with her, but she couldn't find her anywhere. That was because Olivia was up in the flat reading an e-mail from Jack:

Hi Liv, hope you and Eel are coping well without Alicia. I know you will be. You're both so independent. Do keep an eye on Eel for me if you can, Liv sweetheart. She's still so little. All well here. The landscape is breathtaking, completely untamed; just like you! I'll bring you here one day, Liv. I know you'd love it. Preparations for the walk across Snake Canyon are going well, but the location and the scale of the wilderness is astonishing and is causing the odd problem! We have to fly all the equipment in and it will be strange doing the walk without a crowd to cheer me on. But the director of the documentary says that's why the location is so perfect: it'll be just me battling the elements, a tiny figure in an immense landscape. I miss you both so much, and I really wish you were here, Liv, just as you were there for me that day on Tower Bridge. I'm lucky you're my daughter, chick. I do hope you and Tom have made up, and if you haven't do it, and do it NOW! You never know what the future may hold. Lots of love, Dad.

Olivia closed the message and smiled. She thought she would wait until she'd talked to Tom before replying and then she could tell Jack that the friendship was mended.

Aeysha, Tom and Georgia were drinking hot chocolate with whipped cream and sprinkles and Aeysha had just filled the others in on Alicia's sudden departure for Hollywood. Abbie and Jason Hay, the young actor who was playing Rolf and who had recently graduated from RADA, were sitting at another table in the corner together.

"Do you think they're going out?"

whispered Aeysha.

Some of the cast from *Les Miserables*, which everyone in the business called "The Glums", crowded into the café, gossiping about one of the ensemble members who had broken her contract because she'd been offered a big TV role.

"So unprofessional," said one girl.

"She'll never work in the West End again," said another.

"She won't need to if the TV's a success. But it's not right. Her agent must be a shark. . ."

The children tuned them out and turned to their hot chocolates. "I'm completely whacked," said Georgia.

"But was it fun?" asked Aeysha.

"Brilliant," said Georgia. "But for one thing." She paused. "Or rather one person."

"Who?"

"Katie Wilkes-Cox," said Tom and Georgia together.

"Katie is in *The Sound of Music*?" exclaimed Aeysha, stunned by this news.

"Don't even mention that girl's name," groaned Tom. "I thought we'd got her out of our lives for ever and instead she's waltzed back in and is playing Louisa. I know she's going to be trouble. I can feel it in my ancient twelve-year-old bones." A text came through on his phone and he reached into his pocket.

"It wouldn't matter so much if she was in another team, but it's just our luck that she's with us in Alps," said Georgia. "She's already being manipulative. Really sucking up to Cassie Usher and Jon James. The kids who play Marta and Gretl think she's really pretty and keep following her around, but she just ignores them."

Tom suddenly made a strangled noise. He was holding his mobile far away from him as if it was a dangerous animal that might bite. He looked completely horrified.

"What is it, Tom?" asked Georgia urgently. He showed her and Aeysha the text. They gasped.

"Are you sure it's from Livy?" asked Georgia.

Tom shrugged. "That's what it says." He continued talking as if in a daze. "My mum texted asking what time I'd be back. I replied, and then I realised I had an unread message. Liv must have sent it during the afternoon while we were in rehearsals."

"I can't believe it," said Aeysha. "It's so nasty."

"We all know that Livy can be a prickly, private sort of person," said Georgia. "But that's what makes her interesting, and she's always been so kind and brave too. But reading that text makes me think that I've never really known her at all. It's so vicious, so cowardly, she sounds just like Katie Wilkes-Cox."

"I don't get it," said Aeysha, looking puzzled. "This morning she seemed really eager to make up with you. I was going to lend her my phone so she could ring you to say sorry. But then she'd said she'd changed her mind. I thought it was because she wanted to talk to you in person." She added wistfully, "I'd hoped we'd all be friends again. It's not the same without Livy."

"It is odd," said Tom. "Liv doesn't have a mobile. She's always complaining that Alicia won't let her have one."

"Well, she must have got hold of one somehow," said Georgia.

"What am I going to do?" asked Tom. He looked devastated. "Maybe I should have it out with her once and for all. I'll go to school early in

73

the morning and try and talk to her. There must be some explanation. Maybe Alicia's sudden departure has made her flip in some way. She's always found the Swan quite a difficult place."

Aeysha and Georgia looked at each other. Seeing how upset Tom was now, they were worried that if he confronted Olivia he might end up feeling even more hurt.

"I'm not sure that's a great idea, Tom," said Georgia. "Maybe you should stay away from her?"

"But I want to get to the bottom of this. I'm beginning to think that I don't know Liv at all," replied Tom sadly.

"Well, maybe we don't?" said Aeysha. "Maybe she's just not the person we thought she was. She's certainly made her feelings very clear about us. Livy doesn't want anything to do with you, Tom. And that means she doesn't want anything to do with us either. If you're cat food to her, then, I'm sorry, but she's dog food to us."

"Aeysha's right," said Georgia sadly. "But still, something doesn't feel right about it. I just can't put my finger on what it is. Show me the message again." Tom flicked open his phone and showed it to them. Georgia stared at the text for a moment and shuddered. "I can't believe she'd do such a thing. It's just so nasty and bullying. You should delete it." She glanced at the clock above the counter. "I've got to go. My mum's cooking shepherds' pie tonight. I can't be late."

Olivia was waiting in exactly the same spot she'd waited in the previous morning. She had been there since quarter to eight and had become increasingly anxious by Tom's non-appearance. Perhaps he hadn't got her message? Maybe she had misremembered his number? There had to be an explanation. She knew Tom. She knew how kind and generous he was and she was one hundred per cent confident that he wouldn't have ignored her apology.

She'd been so looking forward to seeing his grinning, freckled face, and sure that he would have forgiven her now she'd said sorry. When he didn't turn up, she wondered whether perhaps he'd had a rehearsal at the Duke's this morning after all. Many of the *Sound of Music* rehearsals for the children were scheduled for the afternoons so as to interfere as little as possible with their academic lessons, but there were a number of exceptions.

The bell had already gone. She had just decided sadly that Tom and Georgia weren't coming to the Swan this morning when she saw the pair of them hurrying up the road with Aeysha. Olivia's tummy felt as if an elastic band had twanged inside it. Tom couldn't have got her text! She waved at them, and was surprised when none of them waved back. She came out of the glass doors and ran down the first couple of steps to meet them.

"Tom!" she called out eagerly. He didn't break his step or say a single word. It was almost as if her just saying his name made him flinch. He walked on past her as if she was completely invisible or, worse, didn't exist at all. Georgia and Aeysha followed, both avoiding Olivia's eye. They had completely blanked her! Olivia was so stunned she couldn't react. Her knees felt as if somebody had removed all the bones from them. She stared after her friends, astonished.

They had gone a few steps when suddenly Aeysha turned around and ran back to her. For a minute Olivia thought that it must have been some kind of silly joke and that Aeysha was going to burst out laughing. But her friend's face was deadly serious.

"Livy," she said urgently. "Did you text Tom yesterday?"

Olivia smiled and nodded eagerly. "Yes!"

"Oh," said Aeysha, sounding disappointed.

Olivia opened her mouth again but Aeysha silenced her. "No need to explain," she said coldly. Then she added, "None of us can understand how you could do such a nasty thing. It's unforgivable, Livy, Tom's really upset." She turned on her heel and ran after the others.

Olivia looked after Aeysha, stunned. What had she done that was so wrong? She stood rooted to the spot, feeling utterly devastated by her friends' behaviour.

"Olivia Marvell, what are you doing standing out here when you should be in lessons?" said Miss Hanbury, appearing from nowhere. Although she was acting as temporary guardian for Olivia, Miss Hanbury was not going to give her any special treatment. "I've warned you before about dawdling in the mornings. Take a misconduct."

Chapter Eight

Abbie and Jason were on stage singing "You Are Sixteen Going On Seventeen". There was a real chemistry between them and they were both singing like nightingales. Even the stagehands had stopped to listen. There was a tiny silence as the song ended. Then Jon James said, "Thank you, both of you. If you can perform like that on press night when all the critics and everyone from the business will be here, your careers will be made."

It was rare to get such praise during a rehearsal and as they walked towards the wings everybody in the auditorium broke into a spontaneous round of applause. There were a lot of people in the theatre today because all the children's teams were there as well as all the technical staff. Tom and Georgia were sitting together in row G with Freya and Mia just in front of them, and Joshua was a few seats to their left. Katie was sitting with the adults at the end of row B. She never sat with the other children if she could help it. When Jason came through the pass door, she stood up and cooed, "Oh, Jason, you were wonderful. Such a star."

Joshua looked around at Tom and Georgia, raised his eyebrows and mouthed, "Such a star!" Georgia grinned back. Katie's aloofness hadn't made her popular with the other children in Alps, although Mia still hankered after the older girl's attention and was thrilled when Katie made her run little errands for her.

"Abbie's fantastic, isn't she?" said Georgia to Tom. But Tom didn't reply. He looked pale and wan. A lingering cold was affecting his singing and it had brought him to the attention of Jon James, but not in a good way. Then he'd been late for musical rehearsals yesterday morning because of a broken-down train on the Circle line. Even though it wasn't his fault, it was a black mark. Alicia was always stressing how important punctuality was in the theatre because one person's lateness could cause disruption for so many. Tom just hoped that the musical director hadn't told Jon and Josie.

"Are you all right, Tom?" asked Georgia.

Tom sighed. "I've been better. Oh, Georgia, did you see Liv this morning in school? She looks like I feel. Dreadful. I feel like a complete snake for ignoring her all the time. Maybe it's time to start talking and have it out with her. . ."

Georgia nudged Tom. Katie had slipped into the row behind them. Tom broke off what he was saying. Katie was the last person he wanted to know about his falling-out with Liv. She'd enjoy it far too much. Katie had moved by, but the moment had passed and Abbie came and sat down next to them. She looked concerned by Tom's pale face.

"You don't look good, Tom. Is everything OK?" Tom nodded mutely. "Well, there's something going round. Some of the kids in the other teams have got a nasty bug." She leaned forward: "I shouldn't say this, but it means that Alps is in with a big chance of doing the press night, which would be brilliant! Everyone wants their kids to do press night, all the mums and dads and their stage schools, and of course only one team can. When I was in *Annie*, I got picked to do press night, and when the mum of the other girl playing Annie found out, she punched the director on the nose!"

"What happened then?" asked Freya, who had turned around to listen, wide-eyed.

"The mum got banned from the theatre for the rest of the run. But it felt really awkward because I got all the reviews and Linnet got nothing even though she'd worked just as hard as me and deserved it just as much. The reviews and everything were what got me the TV role in *Jane Eyre*. There's so much luck involved. Linnet's done all right though. She's a couple of years older than me and she's in the *Mamma Mia!* ensemble."

"Alps team on stage, with Abbie and Cassie, please," called Josie. The children stood up. Tom felt under his seat for his stage shoes. They weren't there. He looked around frantically because he knew he'd put them there, but there was no sign of them. Georgia and the others were all up on stage ready to sing "So Long, Farewell". All faces were turned to him expectantly.

"Is there a problem, Tom?" enquired Josie.

"My shoes, they're not here," stuttered

Tom. "I put them under my seat and now they're gone."

"OK, did anybody take Tom's shoes?" asked Josie. Everyone shook their heads.

"It must have been the ghost with cold feet," said Jason and everyone laughed, except Tom who had gone beetroot red and was becoming increasingly flustered. "I know I brought them down," he said.

"Well, get up here, Tom. You'll have to manage barefoot and I'll send somebody from wardrobe to take a look in your dressing room," said Josie.

As Tom ran towards the pass door he heard Josie say to Jon, "He was late for rehearsal yesterday, too. It was in the report from the Clapham rehearsal-room stage manager." Tom had always loved performing, but suddenly his mouth felt dry and he was as nervous as a mouse in a cattery. He took his place next to Katie, just as she bent down to scratch her ankle.

Jon nodded to the musical director, who struck up on the piano and the children began to sing, "There's a sad sort of clanging from the clock in the hall. . ."

Their voices were true as bells and there

was something almost unearthly about the sound as it drifted over the near empty auditorium, which when it was full would hold almost two thousand people. Georgia got a tingly feeling down her spine as she imagined what it would be like to stand in this very spot on stage in a couple of weeks' time and sing the same song with the theatre full to the rafters. It was strange to think that they would all be looking at her and the others. It made her feel very small.

Tom was feeling very small too. His solo line was coming up. He cleared his throat. Abbie peeled off and the chorus began again.

"So long, farewell, *auf wiedersehen*, goodbye." Tom took a step forward, opened his mouth and let out an almighty scream. He hopped around in agony. He had stepped on a drawing pin. The pianist stopped playing. Abbie rushed over to help him.

"You poor thing," she cried, rubbing the bottom of his foot where there was a pinprick of blood.

"It's all right, it doesn't really hurt, it was just the shock," said Tom, aware that everyone was looking at him.

"He could have been really hurt," said Jon, ordering the stage to be swept. "I can't afford to lose anyone from Alps or we'll have to substitute children from the other teams and they're already missing kids due to illness."

"If he'd been wearing his shoes it wouldn't have happened," said Josie tartly, and at that moment Lacey from wardrobe walked on to the stage, waving Tom's shoes.

"Where did you find them?" asked Tom.

"On your dressing-room table where you'd left them, silly boy," said Lacey, ruffling his hair with a smile. Tom looked puzzled, but Jon was already nodding at the pianist.

"We've wasted enough time. From the top, please, everyone." The song began again. But Tom felt completely rattled. He knew that he had brought his shoes down. Or had he? He was beginning to doubt it himself. He tried to concentrate but he couldn't, and when it came to his line, "I leave and heave a sigh and say goodbye," he was badly off key. Nobody said anything and they continued on, but he saw Jon and Josie exchange a glance and felt his confidence crumble even further.

Things didn't improve for Tom the next

day. The children had all been called down on to the stage from their dressing rooms. Joshua had gone on ahead, but when Tom had come to leave the dressing room he found he couldn't get out. The door was stuck. It wouldn't budge however hard he tried. It was as if somebody had locked it from the outside. But he'd never seen a key in the door.

He banged for a while, but nobody heard because they were all down on the stage or in the Green Room, the backstage area where the actors could relax. He tried ringing Georgia and Josie but their mobiles were switched off. He put his head out of the window and shouted for help, but there was nobody about in the small passageway that separated the Duke's from the theatre next door.

The others had all assembled on stage ready to begin.

"Where's our Kurt?" asked Jon James impatiently.

"He said he was just coming," said Joshua.

"Well, he's late again. That boy's turning into a liability." He turned to Josie. "These kids are a bit of a nightmare. I've got one off with laryngitis in Lakes team, a Marta with a twisted

85

ankle in Meadows and Lakes's Gretl seems to be sickening for something too. Go and see where he's got to, love."

"I'll go," said Katie, and before anyone could say anything she had rushed off stage.

Josie didn't mind – it saved her legs the climb upstairs. Katie appeared a few minutes later with a red-faced Tom in tow who apologised profusely. "I'm so sorry everyone. I got locked in."

The others looked at Katie for an explanation but she just pulled a face and gave an exaggerated shrug. "I turned the handle, and the door opened easily," she said.

The others had all looked at Tom curiously then, even Georgia, so nobody, not even poor flustered Tom, had noticed the smug little expression of triumph that flashed across Katie's face.

Chapter Nine

Tom stood outside the Clapham rehearsal room. It was all locked up. He looked at his watch. It was ten past ten, and there was still no sign of any of the others. He frowned; where could everybody else be? The call sheet, which told everyone where they needed to be the next day and at what time, had been pinned up on the notice board the day before as usual. Tom had carefully checked it before leaving the theatre. He knew that not checking the call sheet was considered very unprofessional. There was never any excuse for being late or being in the wrong place. Alps team had been called for the Duke's at 10 a.m.

But early that morning, while he had been eating his breakfast, the house phone had rung and his mum had answered.

"That was Josie Cutwell from the theatre, Tom," she'd said. "She sounded ever so young! There's been a last-minute change of plan and you're to go to Clapham this morning. Ten sharp. You're going to have to hurry to get there in time."

He had quickly gathered up his things and raced across London to Clapham, and had arrived at the rehearsal room in the nick of time only to discover that nobody else was there. It was very mysterious and quite annoying. He had really killed himself to get there on time. He was about to try to ring Georgia to find out where everyone had got to when a call came through on his mobile. It was Josie.

"Where are you, Tom? We're all waiting for you." She sounded angry.

"I'm at Clapham," stuttered Tom.

"What on earth are you doing there?" said Josie. "The call sheet quite clearly said the theatre. Can't you read?"

"But . . . you—"

Josie butted in. "Save the excuses, Tom. We're all getting fed up with this. You'd better get here, double quick. This isn't the first time you've held us all up. Jon is really losing patience."

Tom set off back to the Tube station at a run, miserable and confused. Was Josie insane? Had she forgotten that she had rung his house this morning? Or was he the one who was going mad? He was beginning to wonder. His confidence was in pieces. Only the day before the bag with his practice clothes in, that he'd thought he'd tucked away in his dressing room, had gone missing and he'd had to rehearse in his outdoor clothes, something that had caused comment. Then, when he'd got back to the dressing room, the bag was there exactly where he thought he'd put it.

Joshua had been scornful. "It must have been there all along; who'd want to steal your practice clothes? Maybe the same person who didn't steal your shoes. You're losing it, mate."

The journey back from Clapham to central London was a nightmare because of a broken-down train at Kennington. Tom hurried through the stage door, signed in, charged upstairs and changed as quickly as he could. Then he rushed back down into the wings, feeling as if he had run a marathon. He was dripping with sweat and his heart was pounding.

Jon James noticed him arrive. "Nice of you to join us, Tom," he said, and his voice was so icy Tom felt like a bucket of freezing-cold water had been tipped over his head. It made him more nervous than ever, and he made a couple of silly mistakes during the rehearsal. He had been so thrilled to be cast in *The Sound of Music*, but now he was beginning to wish that he hadn't.

He thought longingly of the Swan where he was good old reliable Tom and everybody liked him and rated him, but thinking of the Swan just made him think of Liv. If only they'd still been friends, he could have told her everything that had happened and how insecure he was beginning to feel. Maybe he wasn't a performer after all; maybe he just didn't have what was needed to make it in the professional theatre.

When they broke for lunch, Abbie rushed over to him and gave him a very public hug of support.

"Come on, Tom. You, me and Georgia, we'll go to the café around the corner together. My treat." They settled into a corner table and ordered paninis and a Greek salad to share. To take Tom's mind off things, Abbie and Georgia started chatting about Katie.

"Cassie's getting a bit sick of her. She's always going into her dressing room and trying to chat. She even marched up to Cassie's agent when she came to take her out to lunch and introduced herself as if she was Cassie's best friend. Asked the agent if she might take her on! Talk about pushy. She's only twelve."

"When she was at the Swan, she once told me that she asked her mum and dad to get her an agent when she was three," said Georgia.

"Oh well," said Abbie, "at least while she's busy furthering her career, she's leaving you alone. I thought she might be spiteful when she realised that you'd been cast and get up to some of her old tricks, like that time she pushed you off the stage at the Swan newbies' concert so that she could take your place. It's good it hasn't happened. Maybe being asked to leave the Swan has taught her the lesson she needed."

"Maybe," replied Georgia. "Apart from the odd bitchy comment, she's given us no beef. In fact, she doesn't really mix with the rest of us. Alps team is beneath her. I don't even think the others like her very much. With the exception of Mia, who's taken a bit of a shine to Katie because she thinks she looks like Sharpay Evans from *High School Musical*. But nobody is ever going to cross Katie whatever she does. She's Chuck Daniels's niece. Josie made it quite clear on the first day that the rules are different for her."

"Ah, Josie," said Abbie. "How are you getting on with her? She can be a bit sharp. But I think her bark is worse than her bite. The rumour is that she wanted to direct *The Sound of Music* herself and felt humiliated when Jon James was brought in over her. So she's been even more bad-tempered than usual. She keeps on getting assisting jobs. Always the bridesmaid, never the bride."

Tom had said nothing during this exchange. He just picked at his cheese and ham panini, crumbling it into small pieces.

"Oh, Tom," said Abbie. "What are we going to do with you? You're not yourself at all. What's wrong?" Tom felt his colour rise and his throat got scratchy. For a terrible moment he thought that he was going to embarrass himself and the girls by bursting into tears in front of them. Abbie squeezed his hand.

"Can you try and tell us about it?" she said gently.

"It's no one thing. Well, there's Liv, of course. We're still not talking. But it's everything here too. Things keep on going wrong and I know that everyone's losing patience with me." He told them about Josie's phone call to his house.

"But that's so weird. Why would she do something like that?" said Abbie, looking puzzled. "It doesn't make any sense. There's no benefit to her in trying to make you look bad."

"I can't explain," said Tom miserably. "I wish I could. But I feel I'm letting myself and everyone else down. And the Swan. If Miss Swan gets to hear what's happening, I'll feel so ashamed."

"She's miles away in Hollywood," said Georgia soothingly.

"Actually, it's a pity she's not around," said Abbie. "She'd sort it out." She looked at her watch. "Come on, time to get back to the glamour and the greasepaint."

Chapter Ten

In the Swan school hall, Pablo and Olivia watched as the children built their structure made from flesh and bone. The tallest, oldest and strongest children were gathered together in a group at the base, packed as tightly together as a rugby scrum. Kasha and his friends Ryan and Jazz had proved to be real team players, never complaining however heavy their load. Even Kylie had won everybody's respect for her uncomplaining attitude and determination.

"That Kylie, she is like a donkey," said Pablo loudly and proudly during one session.

This unflattering comparison made Kylie shriek all over again. "First you say I'm fat and now you say I'm a donkey!" But she had a big smile on her face.

Once the *pinya* was in place, smaller children scrambled up their bodies and on to their shoulders. Then smaller children still took their turn to create higher and higher tiers as the human tower grew taller and taller. Pablo and Olivia clapped as the *castell*, five storeys high, rose seamlessly up towards the ceiling.

Emmy clambered to the top and raised her hand in a point. She was completely fearless, and she reminded Olivia of Eel. Olivia felt a terrible pang; she had barely spoken to Eel since Alicia had gone away, and she missed her even more than she missed Tom and her friends. She remembered what Jack had said in his e-mail about looking out for Eel and she felt guilty.

The tower melted away almost as quickly as it had been built. A huge cheer went up as soon as everybody's feet were safely back on the ground.

"Brilliant," said Pablo. "Your best yet. We'll get to seven tiers, I'm certain. You're all fantastic; it is hard for me to believe you have got so high so fast. You are not ugly ducklings, you are beautiful Swans. I'm really proud of you all. I'd like very much to take you all to Spain to show you to my grandmother. When she was little she climbed right to the top just like you, Emmy."

Even Olivia was smiling, which was a rare sight these days. She was so pale and listless. The only time she seemed to come alive was when she was practising the trapeze, and then she did so with a fever and intensity that was quite remarkable but also a little frightening. She clearly had a gift for it, just as she did for the high-wire, and was progressing at an astonishing rate, but Pablo found her complete lack of fear and her recklessness worrying. It was as if she didn't care whether she fell or not; she had no sense of self-preservation at all.

Sebastian Shaw, the acting teacher, who was now acting head of the Swan, had noticed Olivia's regression too. Sebastian liked Olivia a great deal; he knew that it was her quiet intensity, her ability to experience the world a little more sharply than most people and then express what she saw and felt that gave her the potential to be a great actor. Sebastian had taught Olivia's mother, Toni, and he thought that Olivia might even be better still. If she would only let herself.

Romeo and Juliet on the High-Wire had brought Olivia out of her shell, but now it was as if she had retreated back inside again. Sebastian, who noticed everything that was going on, was certain that it was not Alicia's absence, or even her separation from Eel, but her falling-out with her friends that was worrying Olivia. He wondered whether he should try and have a word with all of them, act as a mediator. But when he raised the issue with Alicia on the phone, she had advised him not to intervene.

"I see it happening all the time, Sebastian," she'd said. "At their age children fall out with each other and then they make up, or friendships dissolve and reform in a slightly different grouping. It's all part of growing up. Olivia has got to sort this out for herself. But she seems to take these things harder than most children. She's exceptionally sensitive, which makes it more difficult to cope with. But she'll have to learn to cope."

Sebastian had seen Olivia and Tom and the others before the falling-out and understood the strength of their friendship. Something big must have happened to terminate it so decisively. But running the Swan was keeping him busy and he had other things to worry about, including a leak in the theatre roof.

Pablo was rather pleased that Alicia was not there to look over his shoulder all the time and worry about the welfare of her Swans. He rather doubted that Alicia would have let him attempt a seven-tier *castell*. But Pablo knew he wasn't making them try anything that they couldn't manage. Circus performers did extraordinary things with their bodies that made them seem like gods, but good performers didn't take silly risks. They managed risk, so that nobody – themselves, their partners or the audience – ever got hurt.

Jack did it all the time when he prepared his high-wire stunts. He would be doing it now in Idaho. Pablo sighed. He had seen Olivia working on the high-wire with Tom, had seen that she assessed risk with a maturity beyond her years and knew it was only unhappiness that was making her reckless on the trapeze. He also guessed that it was only her evenings spent on the trapeze that was keeping Olivia from breaking into pieces.

"All right, partner? Trapeze tonight?" he asked Olivia as they cleared up. She nodded vigorously, and then ran upstairs to check her e-mail. She was hoping that there would be one from Jack, and there was, but it was only a one-liner attached to a picture of Snake Canyon. But there was one from Alicia, too.

Dear Olivia, Miss Hanbury tells me that you and she are rubbing along fine but that she barely sees you because you are helping Pablo or practising the trapeze. You will take care, darling, won't you? Don't take any risks. I feel as if I'm very far away from you and Eel – who Mrs Lovedale says is having a lovely time with Emmy. I'll tell you all about Cosmo and Cosima Wood when I get back. I like them both but they are quite a challenge. When they act they run an entire range of emotions from A to B. But it's good to be back acting again, even if it's on screen rather than the stage. I haven't heard anything about how Tom and Georgia are getting on in The Sound of Music. *Have you? I imagine that no news is good news, but I'll be relieved when I'm back in London in a few days' time and can keep an eye on everything. Take care of yourself, love Alicia.*

The *castell* children were not the only group working after school at the Swan. In the little rehearsal room at the top of the school, Aeysha and Eel were watching Georgia gathering up her things.

"Please don't go yet, Georgia. Let's run through it again," pleaded Eel.

"Eel, I'm exhausted. I've already had a full morning of lessons, followed by rehearsals all afternoon and now two hours of teaching you all the moves for *The Sound of Music*."

"Let's just do 'The Lonely Goatherd' one more time so I know exactly what Gretl does during the song. Please, please, please, Georgia. I'll be your best friend for ever," said Eel, getting down on her knees.

"Oh all right," said Georgia affectionately. When Eel launched a full charm offensive it was hard to deny her anything. "We'll go through it once more, although you were practically perfect last time. To tell the truth, Eel, you're a much better Gretl than Freya. If you'd have auditioned, I'm sure you would have got the part."

"I think I probably would have, too," said Eel, so seriously that it made Georgia and Aeysha laugh.

"But after this, we're going to stop, OK? No arguments. I've come here every day after rehearsals this week so you can fulfil your fantasies of playing Gretl. But it's over. Technical rehearsals begin tomorrow, when we go through everything with all the sound and lighting, and then it's the dress rehearsal, then the first preview on Monday and then two weeks later it's first night – press night – when critics come and write their reviews. I can't wait for the first preview! It will be the first time we've done the show in front of a paying audience. Mind you, all the tickets are discounted because things can go wrong during previews! I've got tickets for both of you for Monday, and there's one for Emmy too, Eel. If Emmy's mum can get you to the theatre, my mum will drop you both off after."

"Oh, Georgia, I won't be able to come!" cried Aeysha. "I'm starting filming next week. Tomorrow's my last day at school. I'm so sorry."

"I'll come; I want to come every night, especially the first night, if that's when the critics will all be there and lots of famous people." Eel skipped about the room happily.

"Tickets will be in short supply," warned Georgia, "but maybe your gran will be back by then and can take you."

"I hope so," said Eel. "Maybe she'll take Livy, too." At the mention of Livy's name, there was an awkward silence and Georgia and Aeysha both looked embarrassed.

"I wish you were all friends again," Eel said sadly. "Livy's like a rag doll without you. She's all sad and floppy. What could she possibly have done that was so awful? She won't tell me. She told me to buzz off when I asked her."

Georgia and Aeysha looked at each other.

"You don't want to know, Eel. Really you don't," said Georgia. "But we're only behaving as she behaved towards us; she was the one who made it quite clear she doesn't want to be friends with us."

"But I think she does," said Eel. "I know Livy and I think it's what she wants most in the whole wide world."

Chapter Eleven

Alicia Swan was sitting in the Green Room of the Duke's with Jon James, Josie Cutwell and the producer, Chuck Daniels. They were all looking at her intently. She had been back in London only a few hours and she was feeling terribly jetlagged, but as soon as she had arrived at the Swan, Sebastian had told her that there was to be a meeting about Tom that afternoon at the theatre and Alicia wasn't going to let a little thing like jetlag stop her from being there to defend one of her Swans.

"Of course I appreciate how serious this is," she said gravely. "It reflects badly not just on Tom McCavity, but also on the Swan Academy. But I have to say I'm not just surprised by what you're telling me, I'm completely astonished.

I've never had the slightest of doubts about Tom's attitude. He's bright, he's always been tremendously hard-working and he shows every sign of being a professional down to his little toes."

"Well, there must be some explanation," said Jon. "I thought he was a really nice kid at first, but he's turned into a real pain. Frequently late, turning up in the wrong place at the wrong time in the wrong clothes. Apparently he also almost missed his cue last night, and he would have done if one of the cast hadn't been right on the ball and sorted him out. Katie Wilkes-Cox is a complete professional. Endlessly helpful and bright as a button. Talented, too."

"Ah, Katie Wilkes-Cox," murmured Alicia. "I'm familiar with her work."

"She's my niece," said Chuck Daniels proudly, "and clearly a star in the making."

"So I've heard it said, many times," said Alicia, imperceptibly raising an eyebrow.

"Tom behaves as if the production rules don't apply to him," said Jon. "It's been drilled into the children that they have to hang up all their costumes at the end of the performance. No excuses. They all do it, even the littlest ones like Freya, but not Tom. Oh, no. Every night this week, when wardrobe have checked the boys' dressing room, they've found his clothes in a mess all over the floor. They're not happy; they've got enough washing and ironing and mending to deal with without him making more work for them. But when he's been challenged about it, he swears blind that he's hung everything up before he leaves."

"I've always known him to be a truthful boy—" said Alicia.

"I haven't," cut in Josie. "He was outrageously late one day because he'd gone to the wrong place, and he tried to put the blame on me. He said that I'd rung his house and told him there had been a change of plan. Of course I hadn't. He just hadn't bothered to read the call sheet."

"Look, Alicia, I'm going to tell it to you straight," said Jon James. "We've already got problems with the other children's teams. Half the kids in Lakes are down with chicken pox, Meadows team has been decimated by a vomiting virus and it's press night tomorrow. All the critics will be there, and you know how hard they are to please. Some US producers are coming with an eye to a transfer to Broadway, too. So I need Tom. But you've got to give him a talking to. He's giving me problems, and I've got plenty to keep me awake at night as it is, what with the stage revolve breaking down twice during previews. We had to send the audience home with a refund."

"Thank goodness for Katie, at least she's always hale and hearty," said Chuck smugly.

"Yes," murmured Alicia drily. "Thank goodness for Katie." Then she added, "I'll talk to Tom. Leave it with me." She stood up to go.

"I'll walk down to the stage door with you, Alicia," said Jon.

When they got there, they were greeted by a rather extraordinary sight. Eel, who was going shopping with Alicia for a new dress for press night, had been left in the care of Bert. He and Alicia were old friends. He'd been stage-door keeper at the Duke's for years, stretching back into the days when Alicia had still been performing. In order to pass the time, Eel was giving Bert the full benefit of her performance as Gretl, honed to perfection by watching the show in preview for six nights in a row. Bert was really enjoying it and kept clapping his hands at her cheeky little asides. She was just embarking on "So Long, Farewell", playing all the parts, when Alicia and Jon James walked into the stage-door area. Eel didn't notice and carried on wickedly mimicking how some of the children performed, particularly Katie. But when she came to Gretl's line, she delivered it with a melting sweetness that was all her own. Alicia was rather embarrassed by the spectacle and moved to stop Eel, but Jon put a restraining hand on her shoulder.

When Eel came to the end, he clapped loudly. "That was great. Who on earth are you?"

"I'm Alicia Ophelia Rosalind Marvell," said Eel, once she'd caught her breath. "But everyone calls me Eel because I wriggle a lot. I'm Alicia's granddaughter." She put out her hand. "How do you do?"

Jon took it and laughed. "She's brilliant, Alicia. Why didn't she audition? She'd have made the cast easily."

"Granny wouldn't let me," said Eel. She shook her head sadly. "I could be making my West End debut tomorrow night, and instead I'll be sitting in the audience watching. It's tragic."

She said it with such a dramatic flourish that even Alicia had to laugh.

Chapter Twelve

It was press night. In just over twenty minutes the curtain would rise on the first night of *The Sound of Music*. Backstage all the Alps children were gathered together in the girls' dressing room. They had been warming up their voices and were now waiting nervously for the moment when they would be called downstairs to stand in the wings before making their first entrance. They could hear the sound of the orchestra beginning to tune up over the tannoy. The dressing room boasted a posy of flowers sent to the girls by Jon James and there were numerous other little first-night gifts and good-luck cards lying on the surfaces below the brightly lit mirrors.

Tom shivered when he saw the cards.

Alicia had taken him out to tea that afternoon, just before he was due at the theatre for a final children's rehearsal. But although she had offered him macaroons and cup cakes, he had barely been able to eat he felt so nervous and wretched.

He knew that Alicia didn't normally take her pupils out to tea on first nights and he guessed that he was going to get a pep talk; perhaps that she was even going to tell him that he had been given the sack and wouldn't be required that evening after all. He had noticed that Jon James had started to frown whenever he came near, and Josie Cutwell was always impatient when she spoke to him.

He didn't blame either of them. Last night, when he'd come to put on his costume, he couldn't find his trousers anywhere, but when he had gone to wardrobe to ask if they'd taken them away for washing or mending, the wardrobe mistress had sworn blind that they had put them back in the dressing room. When Lacey had accompanied him back to the dressing room, his trousers had indeed been hanging over the back of his chair, and he'd had to stutter an apology. Lacey, who Tom knew was sympathetic to him and thought that Josie gave him a hard time, gave a little tut as if even she was finally losing patience with him.

"Is everything all right, Tom? You don't seem quite yourself," said Alicia quietly, once the tea had arrived.

Tom looked at her, his green eyes cloudy. "They're going to sack me, aren't they?" he said desperately.

Alicia knew she had to choose her words carefully. "Tom, I'm not going to deny that you've made yourself unpopular with Jon James and the rest of the creative team. But the boy they tell me about doesn't sound anything like the boy I know. I want to help you, and I promise you that I'll do everything that I can, but I need you to tell me the truth."

So Tom told her everything that had happened, including the disappearing clothes and the phone call to his house. "You should ask my mum; she took the call and she said it was Josie. I *am* telling the truth, Miss Swan, really I am."

"I believe you, Tom," Alicia said. "But it's very mysterious. You're going to have to be on your very best behaviour over the next few days and you're going to have to be extra alert."

She had walked with him back to the stage door of the theatre because she had wanted to give Bert some cream for the arthritis in his fingers. Bert was delighted to see her, and had kissed her hand and immediately started reminiscing.

"Those were the days, Miss Swan. Happy times. You were always my favourite. I used to creep into the wings to watch you whenever I could. I loved your Goneril in *King Lear*. The Queen came to see it, didn't she?"

"She did," smiled Alicia. "And when I was introduced to her afterwards, she said, 'Really a rather unpleasant family, those Lears,' and I could hardly keep a straight face."

Bert suddenly realised that Tom was standing there.

"Here you are, Tom lad, I've got some first-night cards for you. You'd better sign in and take them up to your dressing room." He handed a sheaf of cards to Tom who took them and wandered miserably away towards the stairs.

"Nice boy, that Tom," said Bert. "Much nicer than that snooty Katie girl." Then he added, "Mind you, they're lucky they've got a full team of kids at all tonight. I've never known anything like it. Both the other Gretls are out of action; thank goodness that Freya is such a little trouper. She may not be the strongest performer in the world, but she'll make sure that the show goes on."

Up in his dressing room, Tom had begun to open the cards. He knew they would be good-luck cards and at the moment he needed all the luck he could get. There was one from his mum and dad telling him how much they loved him and how much they were looking forward to being in the audience this evening. There was a hand-drawn one from his little sister, Lily, with a picture of a star on it. There was a card from his gran and granddad who lived in Manchester, saying how proud of him they were and that they would be down to see *The Sound of Music* next month. It made Tom feel very sad. The way things were going, he probably wouldn't be in *The Sound of Music* next month.

There was one from Aeysha saying how sorry she was she couldn't be there, another from Miss Swan and everyone at the Academy and another from Georgia saying, "Break a leg," which theatre people said because wishing someone good luck was considered a jinx. He'd sent her a card, too.

Tom suddenly thought about Liv. He wished she could have been here tonight to see him make his West End debut. He had hardly been at the Swan since previews had begun, but he'd seen her one day earlier in the week and she'd gazed at him with a look in her eye so beseeching that he had had to turn away.

However awfully she had behaved, he thought that once press night was out the way and he was back at school regularly during the day, he would finally try and make it up with her, if she would only let him. Maybe they could never be really close friends again, and maybe he'd never be her partner again on the high-wire, but at least they could stop feeling like enemies.

There had been one more card. His name and address were typed on the front of the crisp, white envelope. He pulled the card out. It was a good-luck card but the word "Good" had been viciously crossed out and the word "Bad" written over it in angry red letters. Inside there was one scrawled word: *Olivia*.

Tom felt sick. He threw the card as far away from him as possible, and it slipped down the gap between the dressing table and the wall.

"Oh, Liv," he whispered. "How could you?"

Chapter Thirteen

It was close to seven p.m. on the press night of *The Sound of Music*. The chandeliers in the Duke's auditorium shimmered and glittered, but the audience shimmered and glittered even more brightly. There were at least four theatrical dames present, and assorted stars from screen and stage, including a former child star who had appeared in a production about which the famous playwright Noel Coward had declared, "Two things should be cut: the second act and the child's throat."

Most of the audience were still in the bars, sipping champagne and greeting old friends with "Darling!" and flamboyant kisses on each cheek. Theo Deacon, a former Swan pupil and now a big Hollywood star who was back in

London to play Hamlet at the National Theatre, was surrounded by friends and admirers. Others in the bar nudged each other and pointed him out while pretending they were really much too cool to care. They all nudged each other again when he suddenly caught sight of Alicia across the room and pushed his way through the throng to her, enveloping her in a massive bear hug.

"Alicia, darling!" he cried. "How are you? I hear you've been in Hollywood, sorting out the Wood twins. I worked with the little brats when I was first starting out in LA. It was like acting with inanimate objects. There are bags of crisps with more talent. I wouldn't work with them again if you paid me a million dollars. Which is what I hope they paid *you*, Alicia, to coax a decent performance out of them. If you succeeded, you deserve every last cent."

"It wasn't quite that much," laughed Alicia. "But I was handsomely rewarded. You really are as incorrigible as ever, Theo, and very unkind about the poor twins. It must be quite a burden coming from an acting dynasty like that. I don't think that Cosmo and Cosima are completely talentless, they just don't have any training or technique to fall back on."

"I heard a rumour they might be coming to London to star in a West End show," said Theo, "but that can't be true; it would be too cruel. You can get away with murder making a movie or being on TV. There are plenty of tricks that can be done with the camera to make a bad or indifferent actor look good. But there's nowhere to hide on stage. The critics would swallow little Cosmo and Cosima whole and then regurgitate them and eat them again for lunch and dinner, too." Then he added thoughtfully, "Unless . . . unless of course they could get you to teach them. . ." He looked at Alicia meaningfully, but she said nothing and hastily changed the subject, introducing him to Eel, who was standing next to her and looking at Theo with awe.

"This is my granddaughter, Eel."

Theo looked at her with interest and when Eel proffered her hand to shake, he raised it to his lips and kissed it, which made Eel gasp with delight.

"You must be Toni and Jack's daughter. Are you an actor like your mum or a daredevil like your dad?"

"Neither. I'm a dancer," said Eel proudly.

"Good for you," said Theo. "You know

what I really miss?"

Eel shook her head.

"Tap-dancing lessons at the Swan. Tap-dancing was always my favourite, but there's not much call for it in the movies or the stage work I do now." Theo suddenly looked as if a light bulb had gone on in his head. "Maybe I could be the world's first tap-dancing Hamlet at the National. I'll suggest it to the director in the morning." And with that he was gone, wending his way through the crowd.

Eel stared at the hand he had kissed. "I am never, ever going to wash my hand again," she said.

It was turning into a wonderful night. The only thing that would have made it better was if Livy had been there. Alicia had invited her, but she'd said she had to stay at home and practise the trapeze with Pablo. Eel guessed that her sister couldn't bear the thought of seeing Tom and Georgia on stage in *The Sound of Music*.

Slowly the auditorium began to fill up. The five-minute bell rang and the ushers tried to encourage the audience to take their seats. The critics, all looking a little rumpled compared with the rest of the glamorous crowd, stood up

119

to let others pass by to get to their seats. One was still wearing his bicycle clips and another had egg stains down his suit. The critics had aisle seats so they could rush away quickly to write their reviews in time for them to appear in the newspapers the next day.

Eel was sitting near the end of row G. She was very excited. She felt very grown up in her new dress, which was dark green and silky with tiny sparkles around the hem and the cuffs. She had glimpsed Jon James in the bar greeting the Broadway producers and had been delighted when he had smiled and waved at her as he hurried away to go backstage.

Eel loved the whole atmosphere of the theatre, the sense of fevered expectation, and she was gleefully anticipating the moment when the curtain would rise and suddenly she would be whisked away to another world entirely and get caught up in the magic of the story.

How she wished that she was in the show tonight! She thought how intensely thrilling it must feel to be standing backstage waiting to make the first entrance of your West End debut. How she envied Georgia and Tom and all the other children in the cast. One day, vowed Eel to herself, one day that will be me!

"Beginners, please." The call went out over the tannoy into the dressing rooms. All those who were in the first scene needed to make their way down to the wings. Everyone could hear the buzz of the audience, which sounded like a colony of busy bees. Josie flung open the door of the girls' dressing room, where the whole of Alps team had assembled.

"Right then, you lot, let's get this show on the road," she said. "You're not on for a bit, but I want you all downstairs where I can keep a good eye on you." She led them in single file towards the stairs, and as she took the first step she turned back and said with a smile, "Break a leg, kids."

At that moment, Tom felt somebody push him in the small of the back, making him stumble. As he fell forwards he bumped into little Freya, who lost her footing and tumbled head over heels down the steps. She sat up, dazed, gave a wail and then fainted dead away.

In the auditorium, the expectant buzz had turned into a rising hum of discontent. It was seven fifteen p.m. The audience had been sitting in their seats for a good ten minutes and nothing had happened. The critics were looking pointedly at their watches and muttering ominously about deadlines being missed. Several people seemed to be trying to make a break for the bar while somebody in the circle began a slow hand-clap but was shushed.

Eel wondered what was causing the delay. Then suddenly a spotlight appeared on the front of the red velvet curtains, one of which was held back to allow the house manager to slip through. He appeared on stage in a pool of light. His forehead glistened with sweat. The audience quietened.

"Ladies and gentlemen, I'm very sorry for the delay. There has been a slight technical hitch, but we're confident that it will be rectified imminently. We would be very grateful if you would just remain in your seats. Tonight's performance of *The Sound of Music* will begin shortly." He sounded extremely nervous, as if he didn't entirely believe what he was saying.

Backstage, it was mayhem. It had been immediately clear that poor Freya would not be able to perform that night, or indeed any night in the foreseeable future. It looked almost certain that she had broken her leg in the tumble. Her mum and dad had been collected from the auditorium by Josie and were now holding her hand and talking soothingly to her as they waited for the ambulance to arrive. Little Freya's face was sweaty and pale and everybody had been moved away from the stairs to give her and her family some privacy. Mia and Georgia were crying and Tom looked completely devastated. Even Katie, normally so super-cool, looked shocked.

In normal circumstances, Freya's fall would have been a headache but not a disaster. Jon James would have had two other Gretls that he could call upon, and on an important night like press night one of them would have been on standby in the theatre. But tonight was not normal in any way. Meadows's Gretl was still trying not to scratch her chicken-pox scabs in bed in Kingston and Lakes's was throwing up at her home in Islington. Even if one of them was well enough to perform, which was unlikely, it would mean at least a fifty-minute delay while she got to the theatre.

"We'll have to cancel," said Jon James over and over again. "There's no way around it. We can't do the show with six Von Trapp children; everyone would laugh. We've got no choice but to cancel." He pulled himself up to his full height. "I'll have to go out there and announce it."

"Mr James?" said Georgia, raising her hand.

"Not now!" snapped Josie.

"But. . ." said Georgia. Josie glared at her.

"Wish me luck," said Jon James, with the air of a condemned man.

"Mr James!" shouted Georgia. "Eel could do it. Eel Marvell. I know she could!"

Josie and the others looked at her as if she were insane, but a hopeful gleam shone briefly in Jon James's eye. Then he shrugged miserably. "No, she couldn't," he said. "She doesn't know the blocking. We'd be tripping over her all the time. It'd be havoc. It's impossible."

"But she *does* know the blocking!" cried Georgia. "I taught it to her. We've rehearsed it at the Swan, and she's seen the show six times. She's like a sponge the way she picks things up. I know she could do it. We'll all just have to help her a bit."

In the auditorium, the slow hand-clap had

begun in earnest and lots of people were joining in. The unrest was spreading.

Jon James groaned. "Listen to that. This show is finished unless we get it underway. If the curtain doesn't go up tonight, I doubt it'll rise on any other night either. Eel's our only chance. She's going to have to do it!" He turned wildly to the cast and the production team. "Tell them to standby to start the overture. Wardrobe! Get Gretl's costume ready. We'll put her in it in the wings." He turned to Georgia. "Do you know where Eel's sitting?"

"With Miss Swan; row G, seats 21 and 22 in the stalls," said Georgia. Eel had told Georgia exactly where they'd be sitting in the hope that Georgia might spot them.

"I'm going to get her," said Jon James decisively. "She's our only hope."

"This is the maddest thing I've ever heard," said Josie. "It'll be a disaster. The death of all our careers."

"We've no choice, Josie." Jon sounded desperate but determined. "The bigger disaster is not doing the show. All our backers, some of the most powerful people in show business and the critics are sat out there! If we do it with Eel

125

as Gretl, we just might get away with it."

Jon disappeared out of the pass door and into the auditorium. He walked briskly down the aisle. The crowd saw him and those who recognised him began to murmur, guessing that something was seriously wrong. He looked slightly deranged.

The director stopped at row G, leaned across several people, pointed at Eel and said, "I need that child and I need her now. This is an emergency."

Chapter Fourteen

Eel hadn't had a clue what was happening when Jon James pulled her out of her seat. He had looked so strange that for a moment she thought she'd committed some terrible crime she didn't know anything about and was going to be thrown out of the theatre. But he'd whispered something to Alicia and Alicia had nodded to her, so they'd gone with the director, who had practically dragged Eel through the pass door and into the wings of the stage. Only when they got there, and Jon James had explained the whole situation, did Alicia protest.

"She can't possibly go on, Jon! She may know all the songs and the dialogue, but she doesn't know Gretl's moves. There'd be chaos. You might as well let a rabbit loose on stage. It's not fair on the show and it's not fair on Eel."

"Miss Swan, she does know all the moves. We've rehearsed them after school," said Georgia. "I know she can do it."

They all turned to Eel, who was pinching herself in case she was dreaming. She was going to be Gretl in *The Sound of Music*! "I know I can do it too," she said. She shook back her curls and looked Alicia in the eye. "And I want to do it, and I'm not going to let you stop me, Granny."

Alicia could see how determined she was, and she could also see the desperate faces of the rest of the cast, all willing her to say "Yes". She nodded briskly and smiled at Eel, who was dancing madly around, unable to believe what was happening.

"Eel, calm down, you need to conserve your energy," she told her granddaughter. "Where's that costume? Let's get her in it. Georgia. Tom. I want you to look after her on stage to the best of your abilities. I'm relying on you both. Don't let me or Eel down." Alicia turned to Jon James. "I hope this is the right decision, Jon. I feel like a farmer sending the family pet lamb to the slaughter. I just hope that you have luck on your side and that Eel can pull it off."

* * *

Now Eel was waiting in the wings with the others. The moment was approaching when they would all enter stage right. Eel felt as if ants were crawling inside her tummy. Georgia was holding her hand. Then suddenly she was being pulled on to the stage.

The lights were bright and unbelievably hot. Her mouth felt dry. The stage seemed vast, much bigger than it looked from the stalls. The darkness of the auditorium looked like the gaping mouth of a monster waiting to swallow her up. She had thought that she would be able to see the people in the audience, but they were just a blur in the darkness.

She glanced along the line and saw Abbie, Tom and Georgia, people she knew so well, but they didn't look like Abbie, Tom and Georgia. They looked like much brighter versions of themselves, as if somebody had turned up the contrast on the TV as far as it would go. Eel tried to collect her thoughts. She had to stop being Eel and start being Gretl. She knew it would soon be her moment to speak and she felt a little sick.

Mia, who played Marta and who was next in line to her, said, "I'm Marta. I'm going to be seven on Tuesday and I'd like a pink parasol."

Eel waited until the laughter passed. This was her moment. She opened her mouth and thought nothing would come out, but to her surprise she heard a voice saying, "I'm Gretl. I'm five," and the way she said it and tossed her chestnut curls like a small pony tossing its mane made the audience laugh.

After that, the rest of the performance passed in a complete whirl. She forgot all about Eel; she *was* Gretl. Josie was constantly with her in the wings, whispering what she should do next and, as far as they were able, Tom and Georgia stuck to her like glue. Everybody on stage did their best to help her, but Tom was brilliant, whispering in her ear and on occasion taking her hand to guide her to the right place.

Everyone, that is, except Katie, who was seething at this sudden turn of events. She hadn't expected Freya to break her leg when she'd pushed Tom into her; she had just wanted to get Tom into trouble. Instead her actions had threatened the whole performance and led to that horrid little Eel girl getting her big break. But there was nothing she could do about it; Eel was being watched so closely that Katie couldn't risk trying to do anything to scupper her performance.

And what a performance it was! This was what Eel had been born to do, and she commanded the stage as if it was the only place she belonged, the only place she could ever be. Watching from the wings, Jon James gradually stopped looking agonised and started not just to relax but to smile broadly. Alicia nodded her encouragement, but knew that her granddaughter didn't need it. She was a natural.

When she ended up in the wrong position in the middle of "The Lonely Goatherd", Eel, Tom and Georgia managed to turn it into a little joke so the audience thought it was Gretl's mistake, not the performer's. It was as if the presence of Eel and her extraordinary energy and freshness had had a galvanising effect on the rest of the cast, who had quite forgotten all about their first-night nerves and instead – like Eel – were giving the performance of their lives.

The atmosphere was electric, and it was sizzling in the audience too. Everyone was aware that some kind of disaster had been narrowly averted, but it wasn't until the interval, when the production's publicist briefed the critics, that the news spread that the child playing Gretl had been plucked from the stalls. The audience had already been responding enthusiastically to Eel, but now they became ecstatic at her every move. "So Long, Farewell" brought the house down, and after that the show – and Eel – rolled on in triumph to the very final note.

The red velvet curtains swished shut again and the house lights came on, but the audience was having none of it. They were still on their feet, stamping and cheering, roaring their approval, refusing to budge and demanding that the curtains open again. *The Sound of Music* was the hit of the season.

The house lights dimmed and the curtains parted once more. The audience went crazy. On stage, the cast beamed and raised their hands to clap and cheer the audience. There hadn't been a curtain call like this in the West End since the sixteen-year-old Toni Swan had played Juliet and broken every heart in the house. Nobody left, not even after the fifth or sixth curtain call, not even the critics who normally scurried away as soon as the curtain came down to meet their deadlines. Tonight they stayed because they knew that theatrical history was being made.

Jon James, who had come on stage to take a bow after the eighth curtain call, stepped forward and held up a hand to quieten the audience. All was hushed, except for the clicking of cameras from the photographers, who had been let into the theatre as the show finished and had been allowed to stand near the foot of the stage so they could take the best pictures.

"Ladies and gentlemen, thank you," he said. "Many of you are already aware that this production almost didn't happen tonight after our Gretl – Freya Graveny – suffered an accident just minutes before curtain up and was unable to perform. Freya has a broken leg, but will make a full recovery. We wish her all the very best. Due to illness, we were in the very unusual position of not having another Gretl available to perform tonight. So it looked as if we would have to cancel our first night. But fortunately for us there was a little girl sitting in the audience who had been to several previews and who knew all the songs and moves. Her name is Eel Marvell."

The crowd went crazy, whooping and hollering. Jon James put his hand up. "I know this is going to sound completely mad, but I'd seen Eel perform a song from the show, and on the basis of that alone and the fact she is a pupil at the Swan Academy, I had every confidence in her. So I decided to take the biggest gamble of my career and put her on stage tonight to play Gretl, even though she had never rehearsed with us and never performed professionally on stage before. I think you'll agree that it's been one of the most remarkable debuts the West End has ever seen. Ladies and gentlemen, I'm going to say something I thought I'd never ever get to say: tonight, a star is born! I give you Eel Marvell."

Smiling, Cassie and Sam gently pushed Eel to the front of the stage, and Jon James took her hand and raised it up. The photographers clicked furiously. The roar of the audience was so loud that it could be heard out in the street. Eel beamed and bowed and bowed and beamed. It had been her bestest day ever, and now she was going to the first-night party too! Life couldn't get better than that. She just wished that Livy had been here to see her and share in her triumph.

Chapter Fifteen

Katie Wilkes-Cox pressed the off button on the TV remote and threw it across the room in a fury. It was the second morning in a row that she had turned on the TV to find a beaming Eel sitting on a sofa being interviewed by fawning presenters. It was unbearable. What had Eel done that everyone thought was so great? Katie had spent a lot of time during the preview performances fantasising about press night and the reviews that would follow. Her role as Louisa was small, but she was certain the critics would spot her exceptional talent and remark on what a star in the making she was. Offers of work would flood in. Broadway and Hollywood would be knocking on her door.

But in the event she didn't even merit a

mention in any of the reviews, and an interview that her uncle had set up for her to talk about being a *Sound of Music* child had been cancelled when the magazine decided that they would far rather talk to Eel instead.

Katie hated Eel even more than she hated Georgia and Tom, particularly after all three of them had been on early evening TV with Alicia, talking about what it was like to be at the Swan. If it wasn't for Olivia Marvell and Tom and the others, she would still be at the Swan and would have been sitting on that sofa, too. Life was so unfair!

Eel had been all over the front pages of the tabloids the morning after press night, and once journalists had found out that her dad was the legendary high-wire walker Jack Marvell and her mum the beautiful, tragic, stage actress Toni Swan, they couldn't get enough of her. Even her nickname had been a source of fascination and many column inches. In any case, Eel's sunny nature and self-confidence made excellent copy.

Asked by a TV interviewer what had been the best bit of her triumphant night, Eel had replied that it was the three sorts of ice cream at the after-show party, and when another journalist had asked if there was anything that could be improved in *The Sound of Music*, she had said, "It's a great pity that there isn't more dancing in it, because everything in life is made better by dancing."

All the publicity had been brilliant for the box office and people were so desperate to see Eel perform that tickets were changing hands on eBay at three times their face value. Although Jon James and the producers were keen for Eel to do more publicity, Alicia had decided that this morning's TV interview should be the last. She was seriously worried that Eel would get big-headed, despite Eel pointing out that she was naturally big-headed anyway.

Eel wasn't really sorry about her aunt's decision. It was nice to be the centre of attention but all the interviews were interfering with her dance lessons, and besides she had other things to worry about. Top of her list was Livy. When she and Alicia had got back to the flat at the Swan just before one a.m. she couldn't resist waking Olivia up to tell her what had happened. Olivia had been grumpy at first, but when Eel had started to tell her everything that had happened, she had become wide-eyed with amazement and so animated that she was almost like the old Livy.

"Will you come and see me perform?" asked Eel, hugging her sister.

Eel knew that Livy hadn't wanted to see the show because Tom and Georgia were in it. But Livy's response was immediate and generous: "Of course I will. I'll come every single night if you want me to."

"No, you'd get very bored," said Eel. "There are three things seriously wrong with *The Sound of Music* – one, not enough dancing and two, absolutely no circus at all."

"What's the third thing?" asked Olivia.

"Katie Wilkes-Cox. She kept giving me the evil eye all the way through the performance."

"How was Tom? Did he do well?" asked Olivia tentatively.

"He was great, Livy, and he and Georgia really helped me out. But Tom's in big trouble. Jon James and the others don't like him. They say he's unreliable and a liar."

"Tom?" asked Livy, astonished.

"Yes," said Eel, and she told Olivia everything she had heard from Mia and Joshua. "There are even rumours that Tom pushed Freya down the stairs deliberately."

"Tom, would never do something like that!" cried Olivia. "Tom's the kindest person I know and that's why he's such a great friend. . ."

She tailed off sadly, and a tear ran down her cheek. Eel clung on to her. "Livy, please tell me what happened between you."

"I wish I knew, Eel. I know I was stupid and selfish over *Romeo and Juliet*. I couldn't forgive him for choosing *The Sound of Music* instead. But when I realised what a complete idiot I was being, I sent him a text to apologise. I thought it would make everything OK, but somehow it's made everything worse. For some reason, it seems to have caused Tom, Georgia and Aeysha some terrible offence and they haven't spoken to me since."

"What did you say in the text?" asked Eel.

"Just how sorry I was and how I hoped that he'd have a great time doing *The Sound of Music* and how much I missed being his friend," said Olivia, and she burst into floods of tears. "Do you think Tom's going to lose the role?"

"Over my dead body," said Eel ominously.

Despite her sobs, her sister gave a small smile. "I do love you, Eel," said Olivia. She sniffed. "Dad rang tonight. He sounded really cheerful. He's going to walk Snake Canyon next week. Then he'll be back to see us. He'll be so surprised to discover you're in *The Sound of Music*."

"Not as surprised as I am," said Eel with a grin. "I don't think I'll tell him until he's back."

Chapter Sixteen

A meeting was underway at the Duke's Theatre. Alicia, Jon James, Eel and all the children from Alps team were there, with the exception of Freya, of course. She was back at home with her leg in plaster surrounded by cards and flowers sent by the cast, crew and management of *The Sound of Music*.

Josie and Chuck Daniels had just walked in together, looking rather pleased with themselves. Over a long lunch Chuck had announced that he was going to tour a new production of *Dr Dolittle* and that he wanted Josie to direct. Josie was thrilled. This was her big break; no more assistant directing for her. She was going to make her mark on the theatre world. She just hoped that animals were easier to direct and better behaved than children. The meeting began.

"Of course, we're dreadfully keen to offer Eel a contract," said Jon. "Freya is going to be out of action for at least three months and we've agreed that she can come back into the show when she's fully recovered. We're booking right through to the end of next year and beyond. The box office has gone crazy. One of our other Gretls is much better. She'll need a bit of rehearsal and should be back at the end of the week, and the other one will be back soon. But we need Eel rather desperately over the next few days, and she's clearly a real box-office draw, so if she would agree to join Alps team for a while longer, we would be very grateful."

"Are you sure this is what you want, Eel?" asked Alicia. "It will leave you much less time for your dancing."

"I'll just get up earlier to practise. I'll dance *and* play Gretl," said Eel firmly. Everyone except Katie clapped and Jon looked relieved.

"Well, that's settled then," he said with a big smile. "Eel, Alicia – I don't know how to thank you both. You've really saved our bacon."

"Well, it's kind of you to provide so many

tickets for Swan children to come and see the performance tonight," said Alicia. "They're all really looking forward to it."

"My sister, Livy, is coming," said Eel happily. She looked pointedly at Tom and Georgia. "She wants to see her friends perform."

Tom shifted slightly and looked uncomfortable. Katie felt a tingle of pleasure at his discomfort.

"And there's something else we need to discuss," said Chuck Daniels.

Now it was Jon James's turn to look uncomfortable. "Chuck, let's just leave it, shall we? Everything's worked out fine."

"No, Jon, this needs to be sorted out once and for all. It's outrageous that somebody in the cast should deliberately try to hurt another performer. What's more, it could've scuppered the whole show. We can't let that kind of behaviour go."

Jon James sighed. Alicia suddenly looked very alert and the children started to mutter amongst themselves.

"Yes, Jon," said Josie. "We've got to take action."

Jon suddenly looked very tired. "Tom," he

said reluctantly. "It was you who pushed into Freya and made her fall, wasn't it?"

Tom nodded.

Alicia leapt into the conversation. "Tom admitted it right from the start. It's no secret. It was an accident. Very unfortunate, but accidents do happen."

"Ah, but was it an accident?" said Chuck ominously. "We have a very reliable witness who says that he deliberately pushed poor little Freya."

"And who might this witness be?" asked Alicia, but from the look on her face it was clear she had already guessed.

"Katie," said Jon wearily.

"Oh, I feel awful even saying it, Mr James, but I did see him do it. It's the truth, I swear. The last thing I want is to get Tom into trouble, but I know what I saw." Katie looked around at everyone with wide-eyed innocence before beginning to cry. She was comforted by Chuck. Mia rushed over to hug her, while Joshua rolled his eyes. He stopped when he saw Chuck glaring at him.

"Are there any other witnesses? Did anybody else see anything?" asked Alicia, giving the other children a penetrating stare. There was silence as everyone looked at their feet or shook their heads.

Tom suddenly spoke quietly. "It was an accident. I couldn't help it. I barged into Freya because somebody else pushed me."

Everyone looked surprised.

"I wasn't going to say anything," he continued. "I thought it was better just to keep quiet, but now I'm being accused of something I didn't do, something that I'd *never ever* do, I just can't keep quiet any longer." His face was on fire and he looked distraught.

"It's all right, Tom," said Alicia gently. "Who was behind you on the stairs?"

There was a pause. "Katie," Tom said quietly.

Chuck Daniels snorted. "Well, they say attack is the best form of defence. Everyone knows that. You're just trying to discredit her."

"I know which one of them I'd believe," said Josie. Chuck smiled at her.

Jon James looked pained. He didn't want to do anything to upset Alicia, who he really liked and admired and who had been so helpful over Eel, but he couldn't afford to upset Chuck, who was a powerful producer. He opened his mouth to speak, but Chuck cut across him.

"Tom," he said. "It's been one thing after another with you since you joined the cast. You haven't behaved at all professionally, and you've bought the Swan into disrepute. I'd certainly think twice about employing Swans again." Tom gave a little cry; Alicia pursed her lips. "In the circumstances, it would be best for everybody if you did the right thing and withdrew from the production."

There was a sharp intake of breath from Alicia, Georgia cried, "No!" and the other children gasped in horror. Then Eel said very crisply, "You *could* do that, Tom, but if you do, I certainly won't be performing tonight or any other night either."

Alicia had to stop herself from smiling.

"Are you blackmailing us?" asked Chuck furiously.

"Yes," said Eel, beaming happily at him.

"Actually," said Jon James, "I'm with Eel on this. The case against Tom isn't proven. It's his word against Katie's. It was unfair of you to ask him to leave like that. You may be the producer, Chuck. But this is my production and my call."

146

Chuck made a disgusted noise. Jon ignored him and turned to Tom. "Tom, I rated you at the auditions, and I rate you now. Despite everything that's happened, I know my instincts were good. So here's what I'm going to do. I'm giving you a final warning. One more slip, however small, and you're definitely out. It's up to you to make sure that you keep your role. Don't let me down. Please."

"I won't, Mr James," whispered Tom.

Once he was back in the boys' dressing room, Tom started scribbling a note. He finished it and put it in an envelope and wrote Katie's name on the front.

"I'm just going to take this down to Bert at the stage door. He'll make sure she gets it," said Tom grimly.

"Tom, I'm not sure you're doing the right thing," said Georgia. "Why don't you just let it be and ignore her? This'll only antagonise her."

"No," said Tom fiercely. "She's a liar and she's trying to ruin my life. I just want to warn her to stay away from me. Katie's a bully. If I do nothing, she'll see it as weakness and pounce."

Chapter Seventeen

It was thirty minutes before curtain up. The Half, as it was called, had just been announced over the tannoy.

Georgia, Eel and Tom were all in the boys' dressing room. Joshua had gone to wardrobe to chat to Lacey. He was staying strictly neutral in the split between Tom and Katie.

"Look, mate," he'd said to Tom. "I think that Katie is a stuck-up little moo and she wouldn't know the truth if it slapped her around the face. But I don't want to be involved. Next year I'll be out of school and in the real world. I don't want to be on Chuck Daniels's blacklist. He's a big shot in musical theatre. So I'm staying out of it. I'd advise you to do the same. Keep your head down and get on with the job."

Just then, Eel's phone gave a bleep.

"That's Livy to say that she's arrived and so have the others from the Swan. They're at the back of the stalls," said Eel happily. "Do you like my phone? Gran said that as I was in *The Sound of Music* I needed a phone so she could keep in touch with me. So we've both got them now. Although I wish it had fewer buttons. You can do almost anything with this phone. Take pictures and video. Record conversations. I bet you could even launch a space rocket with it if you wanted, or make a feature-length movie."

Georgia looked up sharply. "So Livy's got a phone now, has she?"

"Yes," said Eel, idly playing with her mobile's buttons. "Granny gave it to her before she went off to Hollywood."

Georgia and Tom looked meaningfully at each other. Then Georgia, who had been examining Tom's good-luck cards, noticed that one had fallen down the side of the dressing table. She knelt to pull it out.

"Here's one of your cards, Tom—" She stopped and a look of horror crossed her face. "Who on earth would send such a horrible thing. . .?"

Tom tried to snatch it away, but the others had seen it and Georgia had already opened the card.

"Livy! Oh, what a nasty thing to do." Georgia and Eel looked shocked, and Tom looked embarrassed.

"I didn't want anyone to know," he said.

"Eel, I'm sorry, I know she's your sister and you love her, but she's got a mean streak a mile wide," said Georgia. "It's even nastier than that text she sent Tom."

Eel had grabbed the card from Georgia's hand and was examining it intently. "Tom, what text?" she said urgently. "Do you still have it?"

"Weren't you going to delete it?" asked Georgia.

"I never got around to it," said Tom.

"Will you find it for me?" asked Eel. Tom picked up his phone, scrolled down his messages and opened the text. Eel glanced at it, shuddered at the contents and then gave a little meow of triumph. "This isn't from Livy. Neither is the card. I'd bet my life on it."

"But it says it is," said Georgia, puzzled.

"That's what gives it away," said Eel triumphantly. "Tom, Georgia, look at the name on both the text and the card."

Tom stared at them and a look of astonishment mingled with pain suddenly crossed his face. Georgia still looked bewildered but then she suddenly put her hand to her mouth and drew in her breath.

"I always knew there was something that wasn't right about the text, but I couldn't put my finger on it," she said. "The name. Tom never calls Livy Olivia, he always calls her Liv."

"Tom and Dad are the only people in the world who do. If Livy wrote something to Dad, she'd never sign it Olivia, not in a million years, she'd always sign it Liv. She'd do the same with Tom. I know it. It would be like me calling myself Alicia instead of Eel. I just wouldn't do it, however furious I was with you. Besides," she added triumphantly, "this isn't Livy's number. Look, it's different," she said, showing her contacts to the others.

"So," said Georgia slowly, "if Livy didn't send the text and the card, who did?"

"It's so strange. Livy told me that she had sent you a text, apologising. But clearly this text isn't the one she sent. This is from someone else pretending to be Livy. Have you tried ringing the number it came from?" asked Eel.

Tom looked distraught. "I just assumed it was from Liv and she'd borrowed a phone to send it. I didn't think it mattered whose phone it came from."

"But it could matter a lot," said Georgia quietly. "Let's ring it. Eel, can we use your phone? Whoever it is won't recognise the number."

Eel nodded. Tom put the phone on speaker, tapped in the number and pressed call. The phone rang a couple of times and then a voice answered. . .

The children stared at each other. With a trembling finger, Tom pressed the disconnect button. He was so pale that all his freckles stood out, despite the make-up that he'd put on ready for the show.

"I don't know how Katie did it, and I don't care. But I've got to talk to Liv. I've got to tell how sorry I am. We've behaved so badly towards her. She must be so upset. Poor Liv." There was real despair in his voice.

"Not now, Tom," said Georgia. "There isn't time. You'll have to do it after the performance."

"This is your five-minute call," came over

the tannoy. The orchestra was tuning up. Eel's phone rang. They all looked at it for a second and then Tom snatched it up and pressed answer.

"It's Katie Wilkes-Cox here. I've just had a call from this number but we got cut off. Who is it?"

"Tom McCavity. I know about the text and the card you sent me. I'm on to you, Katie Wilkes-Cox," said Tom quietly.

The phone went dead.

Chapter Eighteen

Katie was seriously worried. She knew that she should never have sent that text. It was a mistake to do things on the spur of the moment without really thinking through the consequences. She'd thought she was being so clever. She'd even entered Tom's number into her new phone so that if he called the number the text had been sent from, it would flash up on her screen and she would know not to answer. She also deleted her personal message in case he got her voicemail. She'd thought she had it covered.

Katie had assumed that Tom would just delete such a horrible text, and as time went by and there was no attempt to make contact, she had relaxed. She believed she'd got away with it and, even better, it had clearly done its job and estranged him further from that horrible Olivia Marvell. But now Tom had finally made the connection between the text and her, he had all the proof he needed in that one mobile number.

First, she had to get to his phone and delete that text; then she had to make sure once and for all that Ginger McCavity was no further bother to her. The best way to do this was to make him miss his first cue. He was on a final warning and he'd be straight out on his ear before anyone could point a finger at her.

She had her reputation to protect; she'd already noticed that Jon James wasn't quite as responsive to her dazzling smiles as he had been. This was a pity because Katie still had her eye on the role of Liesl; she was word and move perfect and was just waiting for the right moment to show Jon James what she could do. She was quite certain that he would recognise her star potential, even if she was a bit too young for the part.

"Beginners, please!" The call went out over the tannoy. The children began to make their way down to the wings. As usual, they weren't on for the first fifteen minutes of the show but Jon liked to know that they were all there, ready and accounted for.

Eel, Georgia and Tom walked downstairs together. Tom was very quiet. He was thinking about Liv. He felt terrible. He knew that the way they had all treated her must have caused her as much pain as the text and card had caused him. He needed to explain to her what had happened as soon as possible. The fact that he knew she was sitting downstairs in the auditorium was even worse. She was so near and yet he could do nothing.

Joshua hurried back into the boys' dressing room to retrieve his jerkin and then set off downstairs again. Katie watched him go. Only she and Mia were left upstairs. Mia was being rewarded for the hug of support in the Green Room, and, thrilled by Katie's sudden friendship after weeks of being ignored by her, held Katie's hand as they walked downstairs. Katie had just been painting Mia's nails pearl pink and she had given Mia the rest of the varnish to take home. They turned the first corner.

"Oh, wait, Mia," said Katie. "I've still got my phone. I need to put it in the dressing room." She disappeared back up the stairs, then reappeared a few seconds later.

"Quickly, Mia! Run downstairs and get Tom. I've just bumped into Jon James and he wants to see Tom in the boys' dressing room right away. Tell him that Mr James says he's to hurry up, so he doesn't miss his cue. I'll be down in just a minute."

Mia scuttled off and caught up with Tom. "Tom, I've got a message from Mr James – he wants to talk to you in the boys' dressing room. Mr James said you should hurry so you don't miss your cue."

Tom headed back up the stairs. The door to the boys' dressing room was shut. He opened it and walked in, expecting to see Jon, but the room was empty. Then the door slammed shut behind him and he heard a click as the key turned in the lock. He ran to the door and tried to open it. But it wouldn't budge.

Tom banged on the door. "Hey, let me out, let me out!" Nobody came. Tom went to grab his phone but it wasn't in his coat pocket. He looked around and saw it crushed into bits under the dressing table. It was as if somebody had thrown it as hard as they could against the wall and then stamped on it for good measure. The sim card was missing, too.

Tom ran to Joshua's dressing table and opened the drawer where he kept his phone. But the phone was locked. Anyway, he thought despairingly, who could he call? The police? The fire brigade? Did being locked in your dressing room and about to lose your job count as a nine-nine-nine emergency?

He suddenly caught sight of Eel's phone, which she had left half hidden under a fallen good-luck card. Tom grabbed it. He scrolled through her contacts. It was so new that Eel only had three: one was Alicia's number, which he couldn't possibly ring. The other was Jack's, and Jack was in America. The other number was Olivia's. Olivia was sitting downstairs in the theatre. She was the only person who could help him.

He took a deep breath and pressed call.

Chapter Nineteen

The final bell had gone and the audience were making their way into the auditorium and settling into their seats. Olivia was sitting at the end of a row with Pablo and the *castell* team. On their way to the theatre, they had stopped off in Covent Garden to watch an inspirational demonstration of the art by a Catalan troupe who made eight tiers look as if it was the easiest thing in the world. "We'll do that one day," said Pablo.

"One day next century if we keep practising," said Olivia.

The orchestra was tuning up.

"Have you turned off your phone?" asked Pablo. Olivia went to get it out of her pocket and, as she did so, it rang. She was surprised to see that the call was from Eel and answered it quickly. She was so astonished to hear Tom's voice at the other end that she almost dropped the mobile.

"Liv. Liv?" he said, sounding desperate. "It's Tom. I need your help. *Please*, Liv, don't cut me off."

Olivia felt shaky. Her fingers were trembling. She was confused. Why was Tom ringing her on Eel's phone? Particularly when he was just about to go on stage. Why was he ringing her at all when he had so clearly demonstrated how much he hated her?

"Where are you?" she asked.

"I'm locked in my dressing room; I can't get out. I'll miss my cue. Liv, you're my only hope. I need you to go round to the stage door and get Bert. I'm sure he'll have a key to let me out. Liv, are you still there. . .?"

There was a tiny pause.

"Yes," said Olivia, determinedly. "I'm on my way." To Pablo's surprise she stood up and without a word raced up the aisle and out of the auditorium. She climbed the stairs, impatiently jostling the people who were still trying to get in. It caused some comments about the manners of young people today, but Olivia ignored them and ran at break-neck speed out of the theatre and round to the stage door.

"Hello, Livy, long time no see!" said Bert with a smile. "Last time I saw you it was the day of the final auditions. Your gran said you were in tonight. But you can't come backstage now, the show's about to begin."

"I know, Bert," cried Olivia. "But Tom's locked in his dressing room; he can't get out."

"He can't be," said Bert. "I keep all the keys for the children's dressing rooms down here. We don't let them have them. Look!" He pulled out the drawer. The keys for dressing-rooms seven and eight were missing.

"Well, blow me," said Bert. "Somebody must have swiped them when I wasn't looking." He nodded to Olivia. "Come on, let's go and see if whoever locked him in left the key in the lock. Somebody must be playing a joke, but it's not very funny. They must know that the poor kid is on a final warning."

"Final warning?" asked Olivia.

"Yes, one more slip and he's out of the production."

The overture had begun. Bert pointed

Olivia up the stairs to the third floor and she raced ahead, leaving him to take the stairs at his own pace. She reached the deserted third-floor corridor and the desperate cries coming from behind a door told her immediately which one was Tom's dressing room. There was no key in the lock.

"Tom! It's me," shouted Olivia through the door. "The key's missing from Bert's drawer downstairs and it's not in the lock out here. Are you sure the door isn't just stuck?"

"Positive," said Tom.

Olivia tugged, but to no avail. "We'll have to break it down," she shouted.

"It'll take too long," said Bert, who had huffed and puffed his way to join her. "These doors are solid oak. They date back to the nineteenth century when the theatre was built."

A voice singing, "The hills are alive with the sound of music," could be heard coming over the tannoy. "We could take the door off," said Olivia.

"No time," said Bert. "I'm going to have to go downstairs and tell Mr James that Tom's locked in and will miss his cue. They'll have to call a halt. In all my years I've never heard the like. This production is jinxed. It's worse than that production of the Scottish play back in 1810 when the actor playing the murderer accidentally stabbed Banquo through the heart."

"But he'll be sacked, Bert, even though it's not his fault!"

"I'm afraid so," said Bert. "They've run out of patience with him, poor lad."

Olivia's face suddenly lit up. "Tom!" she called through the door. "Tom, is there a window you can get out of?"

"I can get out of it, but it's no good, Liv. There's a massive drop to the passageway below."

"Bert, is there a ladder tall enough to reach?" asked Olivia.

Bert shook his head sadly. "It's much too high. We could call the fire brigade."

"There's no time," said Olivia. Suddenly she gave a little gasp. "Tom. Go over to the window and get ready to climb out. I've an idea. We're coming to get you. Bert, I need your help."

Olivia hurried Bert down the stairs, explaining her plan on the way, then they went out through the stage door and round to the front of house. Bert had a word with the front-of-house manager, who initially frowned and shook his head, but Bert was a very old friend and he owed him more than one favour.

The house manager beckoned Olivia to follow him to the door at the back of the stalls. On stage, a nun was asking, "How do you solve a problem like Maria?" Olivia walked quickly and quietly down to the three rows near the back of the theatre where the Swan children were all sitting, and whispered something to Pablo. He looked astonished but didn't question her, simply passed the whisper down the rows. Then he raised his hands upwards as if he were a conductor raising an orchestra and, entirely as one, all three rows of children stood up together and followed each other swiftly and quietly out of the theatre.

Once they were all in the foyer, Olivia quickly explained the problem and then she said, "OK, gang, we're going to build the highest *castell* we've ever managed. Seven tiers. Tom's future career and the honour of the Swan depends upon it."

Chapter Twenty

Waiting in the wings, Eel and Georgia were becoming increasingly agitated. There was no sign of Tom. Josie had come by to check the children were all assembled and ready to go on.

"Where's Tom?" snapped Josie.

"He's not here," said Katie with a smirk.

"Oh yes he is, he's over there," said Eel quickly, pointing vaguely behind her. "I just saw him."

"Where?" said Josie crossly. Just at that moment the wardrobe mistress asked her to come and sort out a problem with one of the nuns. She'd torn her habit on a nail and didn't think she could go on. Josie hurried away. Katie glared at Eel.

"What can have happened to him?"

whispered Georgia.

"I don't know," said Eel, "but I'm prepared to bet Katie has got something to do with it. Look at her face. I know that look. She's got a secret. I'm going back up to the dressing room to find him."

But at that moment Abbie arrived and saw their anxious faces. "Where's Tom?" she asked, looking worried. Georgia burst into tears as Eel explained they didn't know.

"I'm going to check," said Abbie, and she raced away. A few minutes later, just as Cassie was launching into "I Have Confidence," she came back, looking shaken.

"He's locked in his dressing room; he can't get out," Abbie whispered. Eel and Georgia gasped. "But Livy and the Swan cavalry have a rescue plan. Fingers crossed that they arrive in time."

Cassie and Sam had just begun the scene when Maria arrives at the von Trapp family home and meets the Captain for the first time. Outside, in the little passageway that ran along the side of the theatre, the Swan children were making their second attempt at a seven-tier *castell*.

Nothing less than seven tiers would be high enough to reach the dressing-room window. They had reached six tiers at their first attempt but the base had become unstable and the entire structure began to wobble like a human jelly.

Pablo had signalled for them to descend and start over again from the very beginning. An unstable *castell* was too big a risk to take, particularly as, unlike the other children, Tom had no experience of climbing down a human tower and his weight would inflict immense stress upon the structure. Pablo just hoped that Tom's high-wire experience and sense of balance would stand him in good stead. He would never be able to live with himself or look Alicia in the eye if someone got hurt in this madcap rescue attempt. There were no rubber mats to break any falls.

A small crowd had gathered with Bert to watch. Tom was hunched nervously on the window sill just inside the dressing-room window frame, ready to climb on to the top of the structure and clamber down it as soon as it was high enough.

"Base, take your places again, please," ordered Pablo. "This time we're going to make it." He knew that this time they *had* to make it or it would be too late for Tom.

Kasha, Ryan, Jazz, Kylie and the other strongest children moved into position. As soon as the base was in place, Libby, Will and some more children scrambled up over their friends' bodies to create the next tier. In the space of a few seconds the *castell* swelled and grew. The fifth tier rose miraculously into the air and then the sixth tier of children scrambled upwards. The structure tilted very slightly, then adjusted itself. Four more children climbed upwards like mountain goats, including little Emmy. Olivia and Pablo held their breath. Olivia could hear Pablo muttering and guessed that he might be praying. It was just high enough.

"Tom," called Pablo urgently. "Swing yourself out over the sill and then lower yourself very gently on to the top tier. Once you're there, come down with a clambering, sliding motion, but keep it very controlled or you'll hurt yourself and destroy the tower, which would be catastrophic for everyone."

Gingerly, Tom inched himself on to the top of the structure. Once his full weight was taken by the *castell*, the structure started to wobble. A few children, including Emmy, groaned.

The concentration on the faces of Kasha and his friends at the bottom of the structure was intense. Sweat was pouring down their necks. With surprisingly agility, Tom made his way swiftly down the structure. The minute his feet touched the ground, Pablo shouted, "Break," and the tower melted away in less than a few seconds.

A cheer went up from Bert and the crowd. The *castellers* high-fived each other and Kasha hugged Kylie, which made her go quite pink. Tom flung a desperate look of thanks at Olivia. "Liv!" he cried.

She just shook her head and said: "Go, Tom, go! Or you'll miss your cue."

Tom set off at full pelt, burst through the stage door and raced into the wings just at the moment that Sam took his whistle out of his pocket and blew it to summon the children. When Tom raced past her and screeched to a halt, Katie's jaw dropped open, before every muscle in her face clenched in rage. Tom, Eel, Georgia and Abbie grinned delightedly at each other, and without missing a beat they marched on stage and took their places.

Chapter Twenty-One

"You can't prove a thing," said Katie sulkily.

It was the interval and Katie, Tom, Eel, Georgia and Abbie were all in the girls' dressing room. Joshua and Mia had been excluded by the others, and were in the next room desperate to know what was going on. But a couple of stagehands taking an unscheduled break had witnessed Tom's miraculous escape and news of it was beginning to spread amongst the cast.

"Maybe. Maybe not," said Abbie, who had been filled in on what had been happening by the others. "But we know everything that you've been up to, Katie. We're on to you, and you know it."

"It's up to you, Katie," said Tom. "Either you promise to behave yourself and get off

170

my case, or we'll involve the grown-ups and everything will come out – the text you sent in Liv's name, the card, the keys you swiped from Bert's drawer and the fake message from Jon James that you asked Mia to deliver."

"Tell me," said Katie, smiling her cat-like smile. "I'm very curious. How *did* you get out of the dressing room in time for your cue?"

"Liv organised a rescue. She's a true friend." Tom looked at his watch anxiously. The interval was almost over and this impromptu meeting meant that he hadn't had a chance to try to call Liv.

"I'm surprised Saint Olivia didn't let you rot like you deserve," sneered Katie. "You've not been a very good friend to her, have you?"

Tom clenched his fists and Abbie laid a restraining hand on his arm. The call for beginners for the second half was being broadcast.

Katie stood up very coolly. "It's been a lovely chat, but I've got to go now." She walked to the door and when she got there, she turned and smiled. "You can say what you like to anyone you like. But until you've got some hard evidence, you can't prove a thing unless I turn myself in and make a full confession, which is not very likely, is it? The text is gone. The card is missing. The keys will turn up and little Mia gets so easily confused." She paused. "Oh, and there's one other tiny thing that you've forgotten. Uncle Chuck is still the producer. I've heard that he's having talks about transferring the whole production to Broadway. Jon James isn't going to want to miss out on an opportunity like that." She started to walk down the stairs. "Hurry up, kiddiewinks, I wouldn't want you to miss your cue."

"I could kill her," said Tom when she'd disappeared.

"That's how she wants you to feel," said Abbie. "She wants to goad you into doing something stupid so you lose your job. Katie's clever. But probably not as clever as she thinks she is. She'll overreach herself. We just have to keep calm."

"It's true what she says, though," said Georgia. "Her uncle will always take her side, and even though she's as good as admitted what she's done, we haven't got a shred of hard evidence against her. Mia's hardly a reliable witness, she's too much in thrall to Katie," said Georgia.

"We'll get the evidence," said Eel. "We can't let her get away with it!"

"Come on, quick," said Abbie, "or we *will* miss our cue."

"I need to call Liv," said Tom.

"No time," said Abbie. "You can talk to her afterwards and explain everything."

The curtain swished open and then closed for the final time. The enthusiastic applause died away. The Swan pupils in the audience began to gather up their belongings.

"Did you enjoy it?" Pablo asked Olivia.

Olivia nodded. "But Eel's right, it would be better if it had circus in it. She was amazing, though. And Georgie and Tom. Tom was very good."

"He was," said Pablo. "Are you going to go round to the dressing room to see Eel and congratulate them all?"

"Do you think Tom'll want to see me?"

"Of course he will," said Pablo.

"But I still don't understand why he's so angry with me," said Olivia.

"Whatever the reason, he'll have forgiven you now. You did something amazing tonight,

Livy. You could have ignored his cry for help. Lots of people in your circumstances would have done, but you didn't, you rose to the occasion."

"Strictly speaking, this lot rose to the occasion," said Olivia with a smile, indicating the *castellers*. "Should I really go round?"

Pablo nodded.

Olivia followed the crowd out of the theatre and around the building towards the stage door. She turned the corner and came face to face with Katie Wilkes-Cox. She hadn't seen Katie since that day towards the end of last term when the two of them had been together in Alicia Swan's study and it had become increasingly clear that Katie would be asked to leave the Swan.

Olivia felt nervous and a bit like a cowboy in a Western squaring up to an old enemy, although she knew that the only shoot-out between them would be verbal. But in Olivia's experience, words could hurt just as much as bullets.

She went to hurry by, but Katie stopped her. "Well, well, well," she said. "If it isn't the marvellous Olivia Marvell. I've heard about your famous exploits with the Swan rescue service. Very smart. I admire that. Tom's a lucky boy to have such a friend. It's just such a pity he doesn't appreciate you."

"What do you mean?" asked Olivia, her heart thumping.

"Oh, nothing," said Katie. "It's just you'd think he'd be grateful after what you did for him. Forgive and forget, that's what I always say, but some people just can't let a grudge go. I'm so sorry, Olivia. After your amazing rescue, you deserve better."

With that, she tossed her hair and walked on by. Olivia stared after her. What did Katie know? She didn't trust her but, on the other hand, Tom hadn't texted or rung in the interval as she'd hoped he would. Maybe his silence meant that he hadn't forgiven her after all? Her stomach was churning. She walked anxiously to the stage door. A crowd of theatre-goers had already gathered outside, hoping to get the autographs of Cassie Usher and Sam Gibbs. A number of them wanted Eel's, too.

Bert gave Olivia a big grin. "You're a heroine, Livy. If it wasn't for your quick thinking, the show wouldn't have been able to go on and Tom would be out on his ear. Up you go to see your friends. You're going to get a big welcome."

Olivia walked towards the stairs but her legs felt heavy. How would she be greeted when she got to the dressing rooms? She knew that Eel would hug her, but it was Tom and Georgia she was worried about. Katie had sown a seed of real doubt.

She was at the top of the first flight when Bert called after her, "Livy! I almost forgot, there's a note here for you."

She came back down and Bert handed her a white sheet of paper folded in four that said OLIVIA in block capitals on the front. She opened it and read the words: "Keep away from me. I don't want anything to do with you". It was signed *Tom*. Olivia recognised the distinctive way he wrote his name, with an almost Elizabethan flourish on the horizontal line on the top of the T. She made a tiny noise of despair, like an animal that suddenly realises it's cornered on all sides and there's no hope left. She dropped the note on Bert's counter and tore out of the stage door and past the front of the theatre, where an astonished Pablo was waiting with the Swan pupils for their parents to pick them up.

She ran so hard and so furiously, it was as if

she was trying to run away from herself. In her pocket her phone rang several times, followed by the "bleep bleep" of left messages, but she didn't hear it. All she could think about was getting as far away from the theatre as possible and back to the Swan.

Chapter Twenty-Two

"Livy's not answering her phone. I've left three messages," said Eel. Up in the dressing room, Tom, Eel, Georgia and Abbie were puzzled. They had expected Livy to be round in a flash as soon as the show had finished.

They couldn't wait to see her, although Tom felt a little nervous. He had so much to say to her and so much to explain. What an idiot he'd been to fall for Katie's tricks! He should have had enough trust in his friend to know that Olivia would never have sent a text or card as vicious as those. And she'd still been there for him in his hour of need, while he'd done nothing but let her down.

"Eel, can I borrow your phone to try Liv again?" he said. It went straight to voicemail.

"Hi, Liv; it's Tom again. We're all waiting for you. Can't wait to see you and explain everything."

There was a tap on the door.

"Here she is!" said Eel excitedly and she rushed to open it. But it was Pablo standing outside, looking a little bit mystified and a little bit angry. His dark eyes were flashing dangerously. As soon as the last Swan had been picked up, he'd rushed around to the stage door and been directed upstairs by Bert.

"What did you say to upset Livy?" he demanded. "After all she did for you, Tom! She was magnificent. I thought that you'd be pleased to see her."

"But we *haven't* seen her," said Eel. "We're still waiting for her to arrive."

Pablo looked even more baffled. "But I saw her running away from the stage door. She looked very distressed. The little duckling cry. And she was so nervous about coming round. I'm sorry, I've leapt to the very wrong conclusion."

Everyone looked nonplussed.

"Let's go and ask Bert if he saw her," said Eel.

They all trooped downstairs. Bert was just dealing with the last of the autograph hunters and telling Cassie that her taxi was waiting for her.

"Bert," said Tom. "Have you seen Liv?"

Bert nodded. "It was a bit odd really," he said, scratching his head. "I was a bit distracted at the time, because there were quite a lot of Sam's friends trying to get in, some of them a bit pushy. They got upset when I insisted on checking with Sam first. Then Olivia came in and seemed fine but when I gave her the note she looked really upset and just ran off. I was dealing with a really nosy photographer at the time so I couldn't do anything."

"Note? What note?" asked Tom urgently.

"Somebody left it on my counter," replied Bert. "I thought it was probably from one of you. So I gave it to her."

"If only we knew what it said!" said Eel tearfully.

"If it's so important, I expect I could let you read it," said Bert.

"You've still got it!" cried Pablo.

"Yes," said Bert. "She dropped it on her way out the door. I picked it up. It's private really, but in the circumstances. . ." He handed the note to Pablo. The others gathered around to

180

read the few words and the signature.

"Oh, Tom," whispered Eel. "How could you?"

Tom looked at their horrified faces. "But I didn't. I swear I didn't. . ." He groaned. "I wrote it to *Katie*, not Liv."

Eel turned the note over and saw the name Olivia on the front in block capitals.

"Phew," she said. "For just a moment, Tom. . ." But she was talking to thin air. Tom had gone. They all ran out of the stage door after him.

"Where are you going?" yelled Eel.

"To find Liv," he yelled back. "I've got to sort this out."

Chapter Twenty-Three

Olivia fumbled as she put her key in the lock of the side door of the Swan. Eventually she managed to open it. It was eerily quiet. At night it always felt to Olivia as if the building was sleeping, worn out by all the activity it witnessed during the day. She had often thought that if the Swan had ghosts – which as far as she knew it didn't – they would be of an all-singing, all dancing variety. She stood on the wide staircase and listened. All was silence.

She knew that Alicia would be in the flat at the top of the school, awaiting her and Eel's return. She didn't want to go up there. She didn't want to have to face Alicia's penetrating gaze and searching questions. She just wanted to be on her own. She suddenly thought about

Jack. It was Jack that she wanted to speak to most in the world. Her dad was the only person she knew who would really listen to her and try to understand how she felt. He couldn't wave a magic wand and make everything better for her, but he would listen and she knew that if he thought she deserved it, he would be on her side. He would understand her deep sense of injustice and hurt.

Perhaps if she explained everything that had happened very slowly, right from the beginning outside the Duke's Theatre on final audition day to Tom's horrible note tonight, Jack would be able to make some sense of it and tell her how she could make everything all right again. How she wished she could roll back time! If she could go back to that moment when Tom and Georgia had chosen *The Sound of Music* over *Romeo and Juliet on the High-Wire*, she would behave so differently. She would be pleased for them and control her own disappointment and hurt feelings rather than behaving selfishly. But it was impossible to have your life over.

She felt for her phone. The red light was flashing on the front. When she flipped it open it said eleven missed calls. She ignored them, and called Jack's number. She heard the ringing tone, and then it went directly to voicemail. Hot tears swarmed down her cheeks. Even her dad wasn't there for her when she really needed him. She felt as if she was the loneliest person in the universe.

Olivia prowled around the foyer like a caged cat before wandering into the school hall. The trapeze seemed to be calling her. She knew that up there she would forget everything in the thrilling sensation of flying through the air. She started to climb the rope.

"The Swan Academy. Please hurry!" said Pablo to the taxi driver as they all piled into the vehicle. They caught up with Tom at the end of the street and he jumped in. Eel, Abbie and Georgia all kept calling Olivia's phone but there was no answer.

"Maybe we should split up and look for her on the streets?" said Pablo.

"I'm sure she'll go back to the Swan," said Tom. "I know Liv. In times of crisis she's like a homing pigeon. I reckon she'll be on the high-wire. That's where she goes to forget herself."

Pablo was suddenly seized by a feeling of

panic. He leaned forward and said to the taxi driver, "Please, drive as fast as you can. This is an emergency."

"We're sure to beat her back to the Swan," said Abbie brightly. "Even Livy can't run as fast as a taxi, and when she gets there we'll all explain that she's fallen victim to another of Katie's nasty tricks."

But luck wasn't on their side, and the taxi got caught up in a traffic jam caused by a bus that had jackknifed across the road. All the side streets were snarled up too, and in the end Pablo paid the cab off and they just ran as fast as they could.

In Idaho, Jack was sitting in a plane on the runaway of the local airport ready to do another late afternoon recce of Snake Canyon when he realised he'd missed a call from Liv. He was missing both girls enormously. It was harder to be away from them than he had ever imagined.

He knew that he wanted to spend the whole summer with them. Maybe he'd even try to get a little circus tour together if he could get his hands on a tent. He wondered whether he could get Pablo to fix something up. Eel could do acrobatics and Olivia could do some high-wire walking, maybe even some swinging trapeze if Pablo thought she was good enough and they could rig the tent.

He looked at his watch. It was eleven p.m. in London. He knew Olivia wouldn't be calling that late without a reason. He asked the pilot to wait a moment before taking off and pressed the button to return the call. The phone rang and rang and then went to voicemail. He left a message telling Olivia how much he loved and missed her. Then he signalled to the pilot and the plane taxied down the runway and took off into the sunset over the wilderness of Idaho.

As she monkeyed up the rope, Olivia heard her phone ringing again. She ignored it, and ignored the bleep that followed. The trapeze was rigged and ready to go. She climbed on to it and started to swing. She flew higher and higher. She bent and curved her body, sending herself upwards. When she had gained sufficient momentum she let go and flipped downwards so she was sailing through the air with her knees hooked over the bar.

After a few seconds she pulled herself

upwards again, stood on the trapeze and swung higher. She felt utterly exhilarated. She arched her body backwards and forwards, and the trapeze obeyed the instructions she was sending it and flew through the air. She sat down again on the bar, and when the trapeze reached its peak she somersaulted backwards, fell momentarily through space and then caught the bar with her ankles. She swung upside down like a beautiful bat, before using the momentum to swing herself back on to her feet again. She pushed harder so that the trapeze reached another peak, and she was poised to repeat her previous feat, counting the beats in her head because success was all in the timing, when the door to the hall was flung open.

"Liv!" cried Tom.

Startled, and about to launch herself into space, Olivia lost her grip. The trapeze juddered and gave a violent twist, and she slipped. She clutched for the rope but it was beyond her grasp and she fell towards the ground like a wounded bird shot down by a hunter. She hit the mats with a terrible, final thud.

There was a moment of shocked silence. Then Georgia screamed, and Tom and the others ran towards Olivia's crumpled body. She was lying on her side. Her eyes were closed, and her face was lily white and her lips bluish. A bruise blossomed on her forehead.

"Livy, Livy," wailed Eel as she knelt beside her.

"Don't move her," said Pablo, dialling nine-nine-nine on his mobile. He spoke tersely into his phone, giving the address for the ambulance. Olivia's eyes fluttered and then opened.

"Oh, she's alive, she's alive," wept Eel.

Olivia saw Tom kneeling over her. "Tom," she whispered.

He took her hand. "Liv. Please forgive me." She said nothing but he felt her fingers make the tiniest pressure on his hand.

Olivia felt a jolt of pain and she drifted into unconsciousness.

"Can we try and make her more comfortable?" asked Georgia tearfully.

"No," said Pablo grimly. "It is forbidden. She could have spinal or neck injuries. If we move her, we might do a lot of damage. She might never walk again."

"Never walk. . .?" said Tom, horrified.

There was a noise behind them. It was

Alicia. "What on earth is going on. . .?" She saw their pale, shocked faces and Olivia lying on the floor.

"Oh, Livy, my little Livy," she whispered. "What have you done to yourself?"

Chapter Twenty-Four

Tom, Georgia and Eel were sitting around the sides of Olivia's hospital bed. A vase of daffodils, the colour of sunshine, sat on the bedside table. Olivia was sitting up in bed, looking very pale. She had a large bruise on her forehead and a black eye. But she was smiling broadly as Tom recounted yet again his rescue from the dressing-room window.

"There was a horrible moment when you let yourself down from the window sill on to the *castell* and it began to resemble the Leaning Tower of Pisa," she said. "But everyone was awesome in the way they held it together."

"They'll be queuing around the block to sign up for circus skills at the Swan now," said Georgia.

"Are they going to allow you to get up soon?" asked Eel, who kept stroking Livy's arm as if she were a cat.

"They're going to come and help me try shortly," said Olivia. "But it's going to be fine. I know it. I feel as if I could run a marathon."

"Oh, Livy, I thought you were dead when I saw you lying there so pale and still," said Eel, and her eyes filled with tears.

"Don't cry, Eel sweetie. I'm very much alive," said her sister. "Apart from the concussion, the black eye, the mild dislocation of my neck, the bruising along my spine and the ankle sprain, I've really never felt better in my life."

Everyone laughed.

The night before, things had looked far grimmer. The paramedics had put a neck brace on Olivia and strapped her on to a stretcher before racing her to hospital with sirens wailing and red lights flashing. The doctors had assessed her immediately, their faces grave. They tapped Olivia's toes, ordered X-rays and shone lights into her eyes. Two more doctors had been called. Pablo had looked agonised; he felt that he was to blame. Alicia resembled a living ghost, and for only the second time in her life Eel was rendered entirely speechless. The first time had been after the car accident that had almost ended Jack's high-wire walking career for ever.

Tom and Georgia's parents had come and picked them up from the hospital, even though both of them protested that they didn't want to leave and wouldn't be able to sleep until they knew what was happening with Livy. Pablo promised he would text as soon as there was any news, and Alicia said they should take the day off school tomorrow.

"We must ring Jack," said Pablo.

"But what can we tell him?" said Alicia. "They're several hours behind in Idaho. We don't know how bad it is yet, and he won't be able to get a flight until the morning now anyway. He'll just be worried sick."

Pablo said nothing. It looked pretty bad to him. He had overheard one of the doctors muttering about concussion and possible paralysis.

But in the event things had proved far less calamitous. The doctors studied X-rays and stopped looking so worried, and at about two–thirty a.m. they'd come to see Alicia, Eel and Pablo in the little relatives' waiting room with good news: Olivia's injuries were all relatively minor, and although they wouldn't know the full extent until the next day, when they would try to get her up and walking, there was nothing immediately life-threatening to worry about.

"She'll need to stay in for a couple of days so we can keep an eye on her, particularly because of the concussion," said one of the doctors. "And the shock could take its toll. But we feel optimistic. She's a very lucky girl and a very strong and resilient one. Not many people could take a fall like that without so much as a broken bone."

Alicia had wept, and both she and Pablo had tried to reach Jack, but his phone had just gone straight to voicemail.

First thing in the morning Tom had turned up at the hospital, clutching a bunch of early daffodils. Their yellow cheerfulness felt like a reproach to him. The nurses had told him he was far too early and that non-relative visiting time wasn't for hours, but he refused to go away and just sat on a bench in the corridor, clutching the drooping flowers and swinging his legs despondently. Pablo had let him know that Liv was out of danger, but that didn't make him feel any better. He felt that he couldn't escape blame for the fact that she was in hospital. Their friendship had gone so terribly wrong.

In the end, the ward sister took pity on him and let him visit Olivia, who was on her own in a side room. It might, she hoped, cheer them both up. Olivia's face was as long as Tom's. From past experience, the nursing sister knew that most people who survived such a horrific accident relatively unscathed were relieved, often incredibly exhilarated, but Olivia seemed miserable and listless, as if something else was troubling her far more than her injuries.

Tom stood stiffly by the side of the bed. Olivia was lying propped up on a pillow, her hair like a dark cloud around her head.

"Hello, Liv," he said. "How are you feeling?"

Olivia said nothing. She just turned her face away from him and closed her eyes. A tear trickled out of the corner of her bruised eye and she winced.

"Liv, please listen to me," whispered Tom.

Olivia didn't move. It was as if she was made of stone, like an effigy in a churchyard.

"Liv?"

"Go away, Tom," she whispered. "You made your feelings quite clear in your note. I don't want your flowers or your guilt. I just want you to leave me alone and never come back."

Olivia turned her head and looked him full in the face. Her eyes were huge pools, black and hard like granite. "I thought that you and me, and Georgia and Aeysha were real friends. But I was so wrong. I've been lying here thinking about it. Maybe I don't know what friendship is. I've not had much practice, what with all the travelling I've done with the circus. Maybe what we had was just a temporary alliance like those people we learn about in history. Maybe we were just all useful to each other. Maybe that's why it fell apart so easily. It's like a *castell*. It has to be strong at the base, otherwise it just wobbles and crumbles away. Anyway, whatever it was, it's over now. Destroyed."

Tom walked closer to the bed. She flinched as he came nearer.

"Liv," he said desperately. "I'm going to go away. But before I do I want you to do one last thing for me. And if after you've done it, you still want me to leave, I will. I promise. I'll never bother you again. I'll even leave the Swan if that's what you want. I swear."

Olivia stirred. Tom leaving the Swan was a massive sacrifice. She knew how much he loved it. It was more like home to him than it would ever be to her, and she lived there. "What do you want me to do?" she asked.

Tom took another step closer and dropped a piece of paper on to the bedclothes. Olivia saw what it was and shrank away.

"Liv, I want you to look at that really closely and tell me if you notice anything strange about it."

Gingerly, Olivia picked up the note, holding it as if it was a hand grenade that might explode in her face at any moment. She scanned the words, each one feeling like a needle in her stomach.

"Turn it over," said Tom.

She did. Tom held his breath. Olivia stared at the name on the front and suddenly she smiled, and it was like the first ray of sunshine hitting the sea at dawn on a summer's morning.

She looked up at Tom. "Oh, Tom, I'm so sorry." She frowned. "But I don't understand. The note is definitely in your handwriting."

"Yes," said Tom, "but I wrote it to somebody

else. Then they must have put your name on the front and left it with Bert."

"Who?" asked Olivia.

"The same person who deleted the text that you sent me apologising and substituted it with another saying how much you hated me and Georgia and Aeysha."

"Katie Wilkes-Cox!"

Tom nodded. Olivia patted the edge of the bed and Tom sat down and started to tell her everything that had happened.

By the time that Alicia, Pablo and Eel turned up an hour later, Olivia was transformed. Georgia arrived shortly afterwards with chocolate and lemonade, and the next time the ward sister popped her head around the door, there seemed to be a full-scale party going on in the side room. She was going to tell them off, but caught a glimpse of Olivia's laughing face and just closed the door and pretended she knew nothing about it.

Chapter Twenty-Five

"But I could just walk down to physiotherapy!" said Olivia impatiently, as a porter and a nurse helped her from the bed into a wheelchair.

The nurse shook her head and said, "Not allowed, Livy, I'm afraid. We'll wheel you down to physio so they can assess you and then you can try to walk in controlled conditions. Just be patient. I'm sure that by this afternoon you'll be able to walk from Land's End to John O'Groats if that's what you really want to do. But you may find that you won't want to walk as much as you think you will. Your body has had a real shock. It needs rest, and time to recover."

They wheeled her to the lift and took her down two floors to the physiotherapy department. Eel, Alicia and Pablo followed.

Tom and Georgia had gone home to rest because they had a performance of *The Sound of Music* that night. Alicia had wanted Eel to go back to the Swan for a rest, too, but Eel had refused to leave Livy. She was glued to her sister's side.

Once Olivia had been assessed, her chair was placed between two parallel bars.

"We'll help you out of the wheelchair," explained the physiotherapist, "so you can put your weight on the bars. Then in your own time you can take a step or two and see how you feel."

"I feel fine," said Olivia confidently. She grinned. "I might even do a cartwheel."

The physiotherapist looked shocked. Most of her patients had to be coaxed into taking their first steps after an accident, but Olivia was almost too confident about her own abilities.

"Let's give it a go and see how you get on," said the physio, and she asked the nurse to help her lift Olivia into a standing position. Olivia stood between the bars. If she was being honest, she found she was pleased she had them to hold on to. She felt a little as if she were standing on the deck of a ship in a violent storm and her legs were surprisingly shaky. Now she was upright, the floor suddenly seemed a very long way away. She held tightly to the bars, then after a few seconds the dizziness passed.

"Take your time," said the physio. "There's no hurry. We've got all day if you need it."

Olivia took a deep breath. Now she was out of bed she was intensely aware of how bruised and battered her body felt, and she was more nervous than she ever imagined it was possible to be about the simple act of putting one foot in front of another. Walking, she thought to herself, was like breathing. As long as you didn't think about it, it was easy-peasy. But as soon as you did, it became difficult and made you feel a bit panicky.

Her body – so lithe and strong and supple – had always done exactly what she wanted it to do, and she had never thought what it must feel like to have a body that let you down. She caught Alicia's eye and smiled at her with a pang of sympathy, thinking how her granny lived every day with the terrible pain of arthritis and how Alicia's twisted hands and feet prevented her from doing the things she loved most in the world: dancing and acting on the West End stage.

Still holding tightly to the bars and

concentrating intensely, Olivia slowly moved one foot in front of the other. She paused, then she did the same with the other foot. She looked up, her eyes shining, and saw everyone in the room was watching her intently and smiling too.

She was about to joke that this walking business was a piece of cake, when Pablo's mobile phone rang. Guiltily he took it out of his pocket, pressed a button, said, "Pablo Catalano," and turned to leave the room with the phone clasped to his ear. He had almost reached the door when he turned slowly around, the colour draining from his face. He gave a tiny cry of distress. "I'll call you straight back," he said abruptly.

Everyone stared at him. A frown crossed Alicia's face. He beckoned her to leave the room with him, but Olivia cried out, "What is it? What's happened?" Her eyes searched Pablo's anguished face. "It's Dad, isn't it?" she said wildly. "Something's happened to Dad!"

Pablo nodded, his eyes wet with unshed tears. "His plane, it go missing. Radio contact was lost and it didn't return to the airfield. As soon as it's light they will look for it again. But they are thinking they must have ditched the plane for some reason or. . ." His voice tailed off.

"Or what?" asked Alicia quietly.

"Or it must have crashed," said Pablo.

Eel gave a great howl like a wounded animal. Olivia felt as if all the air had suddenly been sucked out of the room and she was gasping for breath. She tried to take another step forwards, but her legs simply collapsed beneath her and she fell to the ground.

Chapter Twenty-Six

Eel was sitting on the roof of the Duke's Theatre staring out over London. She'd wanted to be alone, and it was surprisingly hard to find somewhere to be on your own in a theatre as late afternoon turned to early evening. Wardrobe were bustling in and out of the dressing rooms with freshly laundered and mended costumes, and the backstage staff were playing cards, doing crosswords and drinking tea in the Green Room.

She had wandered through the maze of backstage corridors and found the little staircase that led up to the roof. It was dark and dingy, but Eel felt that there was also something a bit magical about it, like the staircase the princess in *The Sleeping Beauty* climbs before discovering the old woman with her spinning wheel in a forgotten room right at the top of the castle. There was no little room at the top of the Duke's, but there was a solid steel door and, much to Eel's surprise, there was a key in the lock. She had struggled to turn it but eventually it had clicked, although the door itself was so heavy that she had to push with all her might before it swung open.

When she stepped out on to the roof, it felt as if she had found her own secret magic place. The city was spread out as far as the eye could see, winking and twinkling like a giant funfair. She peered over the edge of the balustrade, careful not to get too close; it fell away to a narrow ledge about three metres below where somebody had chucked an old roll of carpet.

The night was particularly mild. It was cloudy and there were no stars in the sky. But the city shimmered and glittered as if trying to make up for it. Down below in the streets she knew that people would be laughing and smiling as they began their evenings. But Eel didn't feel that there was anything in her life to smile about.

She looked across the alleyway to the roof

of the Royal Vic Theatre below her. Its roof had been enclosed by a waist-high wall, decked over and turned into a bar and restaurant, and as she looked down on it she could see it beginning to fill up with chattering pre-theatre diners, unaware they were being spied on from the neighbouring roof. Eel moved back; with the exception of Livy, who she wanted to be with whenever she could, Eel wanted to get away from people.

Alicia had tried to persuade Eel to withdraw, at least temporarily, from *The Sound of Music*, but Eel knew she was better off performing; otherwise she would just spend all her time waiting. Waiting for news of Jack; waiting for Olivia to get better; waiting for all the waiting to stop.

But people found it difficult to look her in the eye. Even Tom and Georgia were treating her differently, talking to her in hushed voices and with serious faces. Over Christmas she had gone to the Victoria and Albert Museum with Livy and Jack and seen an ancient Ming vase that Jack had told them was so fragile it couldn't be touched. Now Eel felt that people were treating her like that vase and behaving as if she might shatter into a million pieces at any moment.

But Eel knew that she was strong. She was stronger than her sister, who was lying not far away in her hospital bed, her face and spirit turned against the world. Livy was the shattered vase, not her. Livy hadn't walked a step since she had collapsed in the physiotherapy department on hearing the news of the disappearance of Jack's plane. It was as if everything that had happened, culminating in the terrible news from Idaho, had broken Livy. And Eel knew exactly who was to blame. She sat in the darkness, brooding. She was going to get Katie Wilkes-Cox to face up to what she'd done if it was the last thing she did.

Alicia and Pablo were having a meeting with Olivia's doctor. After Olivia had been picked up off the floor of the physiotherapy department, she had sunk back into her wheelchair and refused to budge.

"We've run every test," said the doctor, "and we can't find anything seriously physically wrong with her that would explain her apparent inability to walk since her collapse in the physiotherapy department."

"That's *magnifico* news," said Pablo.

"It's not quite that simple," said the doctor slowly. "Things like this can happen after a great shock. There's nothing physically wrong with Olivia and we just have to hope that in time, and with some good news about her father, she'll try to walk again. It's not that Olivia can't walk. It's that she's decided she doesn't *want* to walk."

"But she will eventually walk again? She won't be in a wheelchair for the rest of her life?" asked Alicia, looking distressed. Livy was the last person she could imagine confined to a wheelchair. She was always such a physical person, never happier than when she was pushing herself and her body to the limits.

"If there's no physical reason why not, then of course it's perfectly possible, indeed likely, that Olivia will walk again. But the mind is a funny thing. Clearly shock has played a part; hearing that her father is missing just as she was trying to take her first steps may have linked that trauma with walking in her mind. In the end, it's up to Olivia. She's got to want to walk, and she's got to have a reason for doing it," said the doctor. "I think it will happen, but I just can't tell you when. It could be tomorrow.

But you have to prepare yourselves for the fact that it could be years, and it might be never."

Alicia and Pablo stared at each other, horrified.

"I take it that there's no news of Jack Marvell?" asked the doctor gently.

Pablo shook his head. "They're still searching, but the plane has vanished."

Alicia shook her head sadly. "We're running out of time and hope."

Chapter Twenty-Seven

Katie had been subdued since hearing of Olivia's accident. She was worried that if the note she had sent her was found, someone might make a connection between her and Olivia's fall. Not that it was anything to do with her, of course; she couldn't be held accountable if Olivia was stupid enough to go trapezing in the middle of the night.

The accident, along with Jack's disappearance, had become the talk of the theatre. Everyone felt really sorry for Eel. Katie had given up, temporarily at least, on her attempts to make the Swans' lives a misery, and was trying to keep her head down. She just hoped that Tom and the others had too much else to worry about besides her; in any case, she had destroyed the phone with the text and the card, so there was no evidence. Nobody could prove a thing. She was safe.

But today Katie was holding court in the girls' dressing room. After the matinée, Katie's dad and Chuck Daniels had walked into the dressing room without even knocking with armfuls of flowers for her. Eel and Georgia were still taking off their make-up. Mia had already been picked up by her mum, who was taking her out to tea before the evening performance.

"You were fantastic, kitten; top-of-the-bill stuff," boomed Katie's dad, not even acknowledging Eel and Georgia. He and Chuck made it perfectly obvious that they wanted the dressing room to themselves.

Georgia was in a hurry; she and Tom were going to the hospital. Pablo was waiting for them at the stage door. They were planning to bring Olivia back to the theatre to see the evening performance. Eel hoped they were successful. She wasn't sure if Livy would come, but she hoped she would because they were arranging a big surprise for her.

Even thinking of Livy made Eel's eyes well up. Her sister lay in her hospital bed in silent misery, insisting that the blinds were kept drawn so that the room was dark and gloomy. Eel didn't mind. She was happy just to sit, gently stroking the inside of Livy's elbow with her finger. That morning, after they had sat in silence for almost an hour and Olivia had had her eyes closed for so long that Eel thought she'd fallen asleep, Olivia had suddenly said, "He's not dead, Eel. Everyone thinks he's dead. But if he was, I'd know it. Inside. He's going to come back. I know he is."

Eel had looked up to see Alicia standing in the doorway, her shoulders heaving with silent sobs.

Chuck's loud voice jolted Eel out of her reverie. "We've got a big surprise for you, Katie," he said. "Warner Huffington the Fourth, a big Hollywood casting agent I met once, is in town looking for new British talent. I didn't know he was over, but I spotted him in the theatre this afternoon and told him that he really should meet you. I wouldn't take no for an answer. He just had to make a few calls, then he'll be on his way up."

"Kitten," added Mr Wilkes-Cox, "Chuck says he's casting a big Hollywood movie with

Theo Deacon in the lead and is looking for a British teenager and a girl aged around eight. This is your big break, so I want you to shine like the little star you are. Put on your prettiest dress and your biggest smile. Hollywood here we come!"

Eel and Georgia didn't stick around to listen to any more; they both felt in danger of throwing up all over the dressing room. They ran downstairs to the stage door. Pablo was waiting with Tom, holding a battered suitcase in his hand which he handed to Eel.

"I hope so much this works, Eel," he said. "You have cleared it with Jon James?"

Eel nodded. "He said he was delighted to do anything he could to help, and the stagehands did as well," she said. "If anything is going to get Olivia out of that wheelchair, it will be this. I'm certain. Did you put the safety harnesses in?"

Pablo nodded. "Two," he said.

"Good," said Tom, "because after all this time, it might be me who needs one."

When Eel had finished organising everything with the stagehands, she went to get something from the dressing room. Katie, her dad and uncle were still in there. The American casting agent had obviously arrived. She could hear Katie gushing through the half-open door.

"Of course, it can be quite hard working with so many much less experienced and talented children, but I do my very best to help them all out as much as I can."

"She does," said Chuck. "Katie is obviously already a mature talent. I shouldn't say anything, but I think there's every chance that she'll get to take over as Liesl at some point in the run. Although of course she's got lots of other offers."

"I'm sure she has," came the American voice. "Well, I'm sorry, I don't want to appear rude, but I have to scoot. I have an urgent appointment. It's been interesting meeting you."

"Don't go yet," said Mr Wilkes-Cox.

"Afraid I must," said the American.

"I'll give you my mobile number, Warner," said Katie quickly. "Then you'll be able to contact me directly if anything comes up that you think I might be suitable for. I hear you're casting a Theo Deacon movie."

Eel couldn't believe how pushy Katie was being. She wasn't even in the room and she still felt embarrassed for her. Katie sounded almost desperate.

Eel crept away. She wanted to go out on the roof but it was drizzling, so she walked a little way down the stairs and sat down. She had only been there a few minutes when a man with red hair and an open, freckled face that reminded her of Tom's walked past. He turned back to smile at her, a dazzling, white-toothed grin, and passed on. But he had only gone a few steps when he turned back and sat down next to her.

"You're Eel Marvell, aren't you?" he said in an American accent. Eel nodded, her chestnut curls bouncing.

The man held out his hand. "I'm Warner Huffington the Fourth," he said.

Eel took his hand and laughed.

"Don't you like my name?" he asked, but he sounded very friendly.

"It's a very grand name," said Eel, "but it sounds so silly."

"You're right, it is. It's completely preposterous, which is why my friends call me Huff." The American paused and his eyes twinkled. "But, of course, you laughing at my name is like the pot calling the kettle black."

"Why?" asked Eel, interested.

"Because Eel is the silliest name *I've* ever heard." Eel began to look very indignant, but Huff continued, "Or at least it would be if it didn't suit you so well. You can't be more than eight but you've already grown into your name; I'm still waiting to grow into mine."

"I don't think anyone could ever grow into being called Warner Huffington the Fourth," said Eel. "At least, not until they were a hundred and two and very crinkly."

"You're right. You'd better call me Huff, then, because I think we're going to be friends."

"I think we are, too," said Eel, "so you can call me Eel."

"That's settled," said Huff. They sat in silence for a moment, a nice companionable silence, and then Huff said, "I'm so sorry to hear about your dad, Eel. I met the Great Marvello once. He's a great guy, a bit of a hero of mine. He's a dad to be proud of, and I bet he's proud of you, too."

Over the last few days, many people had expressed their sympathy to Eel about her father, almost all of them referring to him in the past tense as if he was definitely dead. Huff talked about Jack as if he thought that he was alive and

215

might appear at any moment. Just like Livy.

Eel liked Huff more and more, although she wasn't sure it felt right to like somebody who was going to turn Katie Wilkes-Cox into a movie star. It was bad enough to see Katie smiling and simpering her way through *The Sound of Music* while Olivia was lying in a hospital bed unable to walk; it would be even worse to see her in a movie.

"Are you going to cast Katie Wilkes-Cox in a film?" asked Eel.

"I doubt it. I just got collared by her uncle who insisted I come and say hello to her; he wouldn't take no for an answer. You mustn't tell anyone yet, but I really came to take a look at Abbie Cardew. A colleague tipped me off that Abbie was exceptional and she was right. I think she's awesome. I'm going to get her over to LA for a screen test."

"You should," said Eel. "She's lovely."

"And of course there's somebody else I'm interested in."

"Who?" asked Eel.

"You," said Huff.

Eel shook her head in surprise. "I don't want to be in the movies. I want to learn to dance properly. I've enjoyed doing *The Sound of Music*, but my gran's right – if I really want to be a great dancer I've got to practise and practise and not get distracted by other things."

"Then that's what you should do," said Huff. "I like a girl who knows her own mind." He handed her his card. "But take this just in case. If I can ever do anything for you, just call. I'll be happy to help Jack Marvell's little girl."

There was the sound of footsteps behind them. They turned and looked upwards as Katie came into view. An expression of annoyance flitted across her face when she saw Huff with Eel, but she quickly rearranged her features into a smile.

"It was lovely to meet you, Warner. I do hope you'll be in touch very soon," she said, and just before she turned the corner she craned her neck backwards to give him a dazzling smile.

Chapter Twenty-Eight

Pablo and the taxi driver eased Olivia's wheelchair out of the cab. The journey from the hospital to the Duke's had been tense. Olivia hadn't wanted to get up and go to the theatre, but Pablo had insisted, and when Tom had said that Eel would be really disappointed if Liv didn't come to the performance tonight, Olivia had finally relented. But she had said very little and just looked morosely out of the window of the taxi.

At one point they stopped at traffic lights right outside a Tube station where people were handing out copies of the evening newspaper. The headline read "All Hope Fades for Missing Stunt Ace". There was a picture of a laughing Jack underneath. Georgia had tried to draw

Olivia's attention away to something else, but Olivia just made a sound as if somebody was sticking a pin into her heart with agonising slowness.

They had wheeled Olivia through the stage door and left her to chat to Bert, although in reality it was Bert who did all the chatting. He told her his favourite stories – about the actress who insisted on taking her beloved Pekinese dog on stage hidden in her handbag until it had got out one evening and pooped all over the tragic deathbed scene, and the theatrical knight whose memory was so poor that he had to have all his lines pasted on to the furniture and props around the stage.

After a few minutes Eel had appeared and hugged Olivia. "We've got a surprise for you," she said excitedly.

"A surprise?" said Olivia listlessly. "I don't think I'm up to any more surprises. I've had enough surprises to last me a lifetime."

"You'll like this one," said Eel, and she wheeled Olivia through the wings and on to the stage. For just a second, Olivia's eyes brightened. Stretched across the stage at shoulder height was her old wire and standing in the middle of it, bouncing lightly on his toes, was Tom. He took a few steps.

"Not like that," said Olivia. "Have you forgotten everything I taught you?"

"Not quite everything," said Tom. "But it's been such a long time that I'm going to need your help, Liv, if I'm going to get back to my best."

"Well, straighten your back and lift your chin for a start," said Olivia.

Eel and Pablo looked at each and grinned. This was the most animated they had seen Livy since the morning after the accident. Maybe the plan was working? Olivia directed Tom for a few minutes, putting him through a series of manoeuvres. After a while he said very casually, "Liv, it's not the same up here without my partner. Why don't you join me?" He held out his hand. "We've got a safety harness if it would help."

A series of emotions flitted across Olivia's face: shock, anguish, maybe the tiniest flicker of hope. Everyone held their breath. Her hands gripped the sides of her wheelchair, the knuckles white. She lifted herself a little way out of the chair as if she was going to stand up, and then she sank back again and burst out, "I can't! I just can't do it! Don't try and make me. It's a trick to get me walking again. But I can't do it. I'll never do it. My high-wire days are over." Then she burst into angry, noisy tears.

Tom jumped down from the wire and came and took her hand. "It's all right, Liv. Nobody is going to make you do anything you don't want to do. But as far as I'm concerned, whatever happens, we'll always be a double act."

"A triple act," said Georgia, taking her other hand, "and a quad when Aeysha's back, which she will be very soon."

Eel and Georgia were standing on the roof of the Duke's, close to a large mound of broken furniture which included an old wardrobe and three sofas. Alicia had arranged for Olivia, Tom, Georgia, Pablo and Eel to have dinner with her on the roof of the Royal Vic next door, before the evening performance of *The Sound of Music*. The theatre had a lift to take them to the restaurant area, but just as the doors were opening, Eel had grabbed Georgia, saying that they would join them later.

Eel peered over the low balustrade at the

roof of the Royal Vic and pointed the party out to Georgia. Olivia was looking glum and Alicia was talking to Tom. Chuck Daniels and Josie were at another table with Katie's dad. Jon James was there too, at a table with Cassie and Sam.

"Eel," said Georgia, "I'm really not sure this is going to work. Katie's never going to fall for it. Why would she agree to meet me on the roof? She'll know it's some kind of set-up. She's not stupid."

"She's not," agreed Eel, "but she's blinded by all those stars in her eyes. As soon as you mention Huff, she'll be here like a shot. She's desperate for him to cast her in a Hollywood movie. She won't pass up the opportunity."

"OK," said Georgia. "I just hope it doesn't end in tears." She pulled out her phone, put it on speaker and tapped in a number.

Katie answered. "What do *you* want, little Miss Georgia Jones?"

"Hello, Katie. Put the phone down if you like, but if you do, you're passing up the opportunity of a lifetime," said Georgia. "I've got a message for you from a mutual friend."

"I don't think we've got any mutual

friends," snapped Katie. "You only hang out with losers."

"Oh, I think we do," said Georgia smoothly, winking at Eel. "Warner Huffington the Fourth."

Katie gasped. "How do you know him?"

"Eel introduced us."

Katie gritted her teeth at the memory of seeing Eel on the stairs with Warner. "So?" she said.

"Well, Katie, it's our lucky day. He wants to audition us both for a new movie he's casting."

"The one with Theo Deacon?" said Katie excitedly.

"That's the one," said Georgia, giving the performance of a lifetime.

"Are we going to fly to LA for a screen test?" asked Katie.

"Well, he may fly one of us over later if he thinks we're good enough, but for now he wants to meet us both on the roof of the Duke's for a preliminary audition."

"The roof of the Duke's?" said Katie, sounding puzzled. It was a strange place for an audition, but these movie people were all a little crazy.

"Yes," said Georgia. "I know. Insane,

isn't it? But he told me it had exactly the right ambience, or something. I'm already here, and he's on his way."

"So am I!" said Katie excitedly. She wasn't going to let Georgia Jones steal a march on her.

Georgia disconnected the call and turned to Eel. "Is your phone ready to record?" she asked. Eel nodded. "You'd better hide behind that old wardrobe, then. She'll be here any minute."

Chapter Twenty-Nine

"Where's Warner?" demanded Katie as soon as she arrived on the roof.

"He just called. He said he won't be long."

"Well, well, well. It's just you and me, Georgia Jones. Up against each other again just like we were at the newbies' concert at the Swan last term. But I got the better of you then, didn't I?"

"I guess you did," said Georgia, "but pushing someone off the stage so you can take their place is hardly fair play."

Katie coloured slightly. "I never meant to really hurt you, Georgia. I just wanted you out of the way. Just like I never meant to hurt that irritating Freya kid when I shoved Tom in the back. I just wanted to get him into big trouble. How was I to know the silly kid would break her stupid leg?"

"It was a bit unfortunate," said Georgia neutrally.

"It was, because it allowed that dreadful Eel to take centre stage." Katie eyed Georgia. "I always rather liked you, Georgia Jones. You were one of the few kids at the Swan who I thought had real talent. But you'll never be a star like me because you're just too nice and you lack ambition. You have to be ruthless if you're going to get to the top."

"You're ruthless, aren't you, Katie? And proud of it. I admire that about you."

"I admire it too," said Katie, who was starting to enjoy her chat with Georgia. It was good to have somebody to boast to. "I really did for that Tom McCavity. I bet he thought he was going mad. It was me who stole his shoes and kept messing up his costumes, and of course it was me who locked him in his dressing room, and sent him that bad-luck card. I rang his mum too, pretending to be Josie and sent him to the Clapham rehearsal room."

"Wow, you're really clever," said Georgia quietly.

"It only got better after that, though,"

boasted Katie. "A real masterstroke was to take the note that Tom had written to me and put Olivia Marvell's name on it and leave it for her. But of course the thing I'm most proud of was messing around with her text message to Ginger Tom. That turned you all against her, which I really enjoyed watching." She paused. "But best of all is that nobody can prove a thing . . . there's no evidence apart from the note and that's mostly in Tom's handwriting."

"Oh, but there *is* evidence now," said Eel, stepping out from behind the pile of old furniture.

Katie looked around wildly. "What is this?" she shrieked. "Where's Warner? There is no audition, is there? This is some kind of set-up!"

"Yes, it is," said Eel, and she pressed play on her phone. Katie's confession began to ring out loud and clear.

Bile rose in Katie's throat. She rushed at Eel, who dropped the phone as she put her hands up to defend herself. But Katie didn't touch her, she just stopped right in front of her and shouted into her face: "You! You marvellous Marvells. Everything was all right at the Swan until you and your horrible sister turned up. *You're* to blame for this. Not me. It's you two and your awful friends who have made me behave like this. It's all your fault! I'm glad your sister can't walk and your dad's dead! It's what you deserve."

Katie was shouting so loudly that people in the Royal Vic restaurant had started to stand up and look across the passageway to the Duke's roof. Katie turned away towards the door, then suddenly she ran back at full pelt, throwing herself on Eel in a fury. The two girls crashed backwards into the balustrade. Georgia screamed as the ancient brickwork crumbled and Eel and Katie flew over the edge of the building.

They landed a metre below on the ledge, the abandoned roll of carpet breaking their fall. For a second there was silence, and then Katie screamed as she started to slip off the ledge. In the Royal Vic restaurant people began to scream, too. Up on the roof a panicky Georgia picked up Eel's phone and dialled nine-nine-nine.

Chapter Thirty

As Katie slipped over the ledge, she put out her hands and, more by luck than judgement, managed to catch hold of the rusty old flagpole that extended out from the building. She clung desperately on to it, her feet dangling over the terrible drop below.

Shocked but unharmed by the fall, which had knocked all the breath out of her, Eel sat up. Katie was in terrible danger. She leaned towards her, trying not to look down at the drop below, and put a hand out. But Katie flinched back as if Eel had burned her.

"Katie," said Eel very calmly, "try to inch yourself closer to the ledge, one hand over the other." But Katie was completely hysterical; she could no more do that than she could sprout wings and fly.

"I'm going to fall," she gasped. "I'm going to fall. I can't hold on much longer."

"No, you're not," said Eel. "Everything's going to be all right." She hoped she sounded more certain than she felt. She knew that she didn't have the strength to pull Katie to safety; Katie's weight would drag her over the edge, too, and Katie was in such a state that she couldn't help herself at all.

Down in the passageway a small crowd had gathered, and the faces of the people watching from the Royal Vic were white and scared. Some, though, were filming it on their phones. Alicia and Pablo had seen what had happened and had rushed back to the Duke's, leaving Olivia, Tom and Georgia looking on in horror. Jon James, Cassie, Chuck and Katie's dad were also heading for the roof of the Duke's.

Once on the roof, Jon and Pablo immediately started to climb over the balustrade to make a rescue attempt, but the brickwork was so old and crumbling that their movements caused broken bits of brick to fall down on to the girls below. After one brick narrowly missed Eel's head, they retreated, aware that they were in serious danger of doing more harm than good.

Suddenly there was a commotion behind the people watching on the Royal Vic roof. The crowd parted as Tom pushed Olivia's wheelchair to the wall that ran around the edge of the restaurant. Olivia was frantically indicating the wire in her suitcase on the back of the wheelchair. Tom made a face and took the wire and harnesses out of the suitcase.

"Eel!" shouted Olivia. "See that hook on the brickwork to your left?" Eel nodded. "Is it secure?" Eel pulled at it and nodded again. "OK, Tom's going to throw you the wire. I want you to slip it over that hook."

Tom threw the wire across the passageway and Eel caught it easily. She attached it to the hook and checked that it was secure. Tom was looking for somewhere to fix the wire on the Royal Vic side of the gap.

"I can't hold on much longer!" cried Katie.

"Yes, you can, Katie," said Eel. "You've got everything to live for. You're going to be a star."

"No, I'm not," wept the other girl.

"Yes, you are," said Eel. "You're just going to have to work for it and stop expecting it to drop into your lap. But you're going to make it, I know you are. You just have to hang in there like you're hanging on now."

Tom had found a place to hook the wire so it was now taut across the passageway. He came back to Olivia and said, "It's done, and I've got the safety harnesses you wanted. But how's this going to help, Liv? What's going to happen now?"

Heaving herself out of her wheelchair, Olivia said, "You and I are going to walk across the wire and rescue Katie. She's never going to hold on until the emergency services get here."

Tom stared at Olivia for a second, a look of total horror on his face. Then he took a deep breath, said, "Welcome back, partner," and started to help her on to the wall. Alicia, who was now standing on the Duke's roof with Pablo, saw what was happening and shouted, "No!"

But Pablo put his arm around her shoulders and said, "It's all right, Alicia, she's assessed the risk. She knows that they can do it. Have faith. Livy wouldn't do something on the wire that she thought was too dangerous."

A noise like a rumble of thunder grew

through the watching crowd as they realised what was happening. A few adults protested loudly, but others pointed out that Katie clearly wasn't going to be able to hang on much longer.

"Quiet, they're fully trained. They know what they're doing," shouted Pablo. Everyone was silenced.

Standing up on the wall, Olivia felt very shaky. She wasn't sure that her legs were going to obey her. She thought of the time she had walked the wire across the very top of the towers on Tower Bridge and how frightening the river below had seemed. But she had looked up and walked on then. This time, too, there was nothing to fear except fear itself.

Down below she could see that people were trying to move mattresses underneath the flagpole, including the one from the bedroom scene in *The Sound of Music*. Other people were carrying mattresses from a bedding store a few doors down.

She looked across the wire at Eel and Katie's frightened faces. "Katie," she said, "we're coming to get you."

Olivia stepped out into thin air. Her foot hit the wire and instead of feeling terrifying it was like coming home. She was back where she belonged. She took a few steps and waited for the moment when she would feel the wire shake as Tom stepped out behind her. It came. She raised a hand to him to indicate she was ready to move forwards, and then she walked swiftly across the wire, stepped on to the narrow ledge, crouched down and laid a soothing hand on Eel's cheek.

Tom stepped on to the ledge behind her and crouched, too. Up on the roof of the Duke's, Alicia and Pablo hugged each other, even though they knew that the danger had far from passed.

Olivia took one of the safety harnesses that were slung over Tom's shoulder and put it over the hook. "You're going to have to do this, Tom. I'm not strong enough." She put the belt around his waist, clipped on the harness and attached the other end to the hook. Then she passed one end of the second harness over the hook and gave the belt and the other end to Tom.

"You've got to lean down and put the belt around her waist, clip on the harness and then try and heave her up. At least if she does fall, she's got a chance. As long as the hook holds."

Katie had stopped crying and was just

whimpering to herself. Tom leaned down and did as Liv had instructed. Olivia heaved a sigh of relief. From up above came a shout. One of the stagehands who had gathered on the roof had found a safety-wire cable and Pablo was lowering it towards them. Tom clipped that on to Katie's belt, too.

"Right, on the count of three: one, two, three . . . heave!" shouted Olivia. Tom grabbed one of Katie's arms and Olivia grabbed the other and Katie let go of the flagpole. For a moment it seemed as if she would pull them all downwards but the stagehands, who were all pulling for dear life, took her weight and started to haul her upwards. With one frantic, messy fumbling movement, they managed to grab Katie and the next minute she was sitting on the ledge with the rest of them.

A huge roar went up from the crowd and from far away the faint sound of a fire engine could be heard.

Olivia leaned her back against the wall, waiting for the adrenalin rush to subside. Her phone started to ring in her pocket. Without thinking, she reached wearily to answer it and put the phone to her ear. For a moment she said nothing, but then burst into huge sobs. "Eel!" she cried, grabbing her little sister.

"Livy, what's wrong?" asked Eel.

"There's nothing wrong," sobbed Olivia. "It's Dad." She choked. "Jack's not dead, Eel; he's alive!"

Chapter Thirty-One

A week later, Olivia and Eel were at Heathrow airport with Alicia and Pablo. They had just waved goodbye to Abbie, who was on her way to Hollywood with Huff for a screen test. She had managed to negotiate two days off from *The Sound of Music* with Jon James's blessing.

Now they were waiting for the arrival of Jack's plane from Seattle, as were an entire pack of journalists and photographers. The extraordinary story of Jack's survival combined with his daughter's leading role in the rescue of another child from the roof of a West End theatre had been irresistible, and the media had run and run with the story. Some were calling Olivia's act of stepping out of the wheelchair on to the wire a miracle, which made Olivia furious because as she kept on pointing out crossly to any journalist who would listen, it wasn't that she *couldn't* walk but rather than she *wouldn't* walk.

There was a real media feeding-frenzy. Footage of the rescue filmed on mobile phones was all over YouTube, and the papers were desperate to get the full details of Jack's survival. After his plane had had to ditch because of an electrical failure, he had walked for four days through wilderness and dangerous terrain to get help for the pilot, who had broken his ankle.

The Marvells were being hailed as the most heroic family in the country, which made Olivia want to hide away, and made Eel feel embarrassed and guilty. She was well aware that if it had not been for her scheme to get Katie to admit to all her wrong-doings, nobody's life would have been in danger. In some ways she thought that perhaps she had been as sneaky as Katie, an opinion that her grandmother happened to share. Alicia had told Eel and Georgia off so sternly that both of them had been reduced to floods of tears.

But at least two brilliant things had come out of it: Olivia had started walking again, and

Katie was no longer in *The Sound of Music*. She hadn't even waited to be sacked but had sent a letter withdrawing from the production the next morning.

There was a third thing too: Katie had asked to meet Olivia, Eel, Tom and Georgia at the theatre that afternoon when she had come to pick up her things. Katie had looked terrible. Her eyes were red-rimmed, her skin blotchy and her normally glossy hair was dull and lifeless. She found it difficult to look them in the eye and there was an awkward silence at first, but then Katie whispered, "Olivia, Tom, I want to say thank you. You saved my life. You did something for me that I wouldn't have done for you. You could have just left me to fall, but you didn't. I'll be eternally grateful."

By now she was crying, but she continued: "And I want to say sorry. I've been awful to you all. I know you probably hate me, and can never forgive me for what I did, but I want you to know that I'll regret it for the rest of my life."

"We don't hate you, Katie," said Tom.

"No," said Eel very seriously. "We feel really sorry for you."

Katie gave a wan little smile. "Which of

course is even worse. I don't deserve your pity."

"I'm sorry I stitched you up, Katie," said Eel.

"No," replied Katie. "I deserved that, too. I've not been a nice person."

"Hurry up, kitten," called Mr Wilkes-Cox from outside the room.

"I've got to go. My dad doesn't like to be kept waiting," said Katie, and she gathered up her things and walked to the door. Then she turned around.

"You lot have something special: real friendship. Even I couldn't destroy that. I envy you." With that she was gone, leaving the door open.

"Come on, kitten!" said her dad as he started down the stairs.

There was a pause, and then they heard Katie reply: "I'm not *kitten*, Dad. My name's Katie. I'd like it if you called me by my name from now on."

At the airport, the arrivals board showed that Jack's plane had landed. Olivia was so nervous she'd begun to hiccup and Eel was even more hyperactive than usual, and kept pirouetting into people's luggage trolleys.

Suddenly the doors from arrivals opened and Jack appeared, accompanied by several airline officials. He looked tired but he was smiling, his green-blue eyes sparkling like the sea on a summer's day. Olivia and Eel gave whoops of joy and ran towards him. He enveloped them in a huge hug. They nuzzled each other like ponies, repeating each other's names over and over, completely oblivious to the commotion around them. A hundred flashbulbs popped as the photographers vied to snap the picture that would be all over the next day's papers.

A few days later, a little party was just concluding at Alicia's flat. It was late. Olivia, Jack, Pablo and Aeysha, who was now back at school just in time for the end of term, had all been to see Alps team, with Lakes's Louisa, perform in the matinée of *The Sound of Music*. Alicia had wanted to go, too, but felt she had been neglecting the Swan so had decided against it.

Afterwards they had been joined at the school by Eel, Tom, Georgia and Abbie, who was back from her screen test in LA. She didn't know if she had got the part yet, but she said that Huff had thought she was in with a good chance.

"And if I don't get it, there will be other opportunities," she said. Now she had turned sixteen she would be leaving the Swan at the end of term. Alicia, who had been listening, smiled. She knew Abbie would be fine; she had her head screwed on straight.

Pablo was just getting ready to leave.

"Wait a minute, Pablo," said Jack. He turned to Olivia. "Liv, will you have a go on the trapeze? I want to see what you can do."

Olivia hesitated. She hadn't been on the trapeze since the night of her fall.

"Jack, I'm not sure that's the best idea," said Alicia. "I can't imagine that Livy ever wants to see a trapeze again, and I'm not sure I can bear to see her on one." She shuddered. "I can't get the picture of her lying broken on the floor out of my head."

Jack held his daughter's gaze. "No, Gran," said Olivia. "I've got to get back on. It's like horses and bicycles. You fall off and you get back on again as soon as you can. Dad's right. I should go on the trapeze, and there's no time like the present."

They all trooped down to the hall. Pablo unhooked the trapeze and checked the rigging. Then Olivia shimmied up the rope and on to the bar. She began to swing. She pushed her body hard and the trapeze responded as if it was alive. Olivia flew up into the air, and as the trapeze reached its peak, she somersaulted backwards, caught the bar with her ankles and sailed through the air. A great cry of encouragement went up from Jack, Pablo and Eel, who squealed and jiggled with pride and excitement.

Olivia swung her body upwards again and grinned. Below she could see the smiling upturned faces of Jack, Eel, Alicia and all the people she loved most in the world. Tom had raised his arms up in the air as if he was reaching for the sky to try to touch her.

She pushed her body and the trapeze even harder so it swung in a gigantic arc and the air rushed by her face like a great warm wind. She was like a beautiful bird taking flight. Olivia felt an extraordinary sense of release and exhilaration, and as she rose upwards, she felt as if she was flying, flying as fast as she could towards her future and the next term at the Swan.

To find out about further titles in the

Olivia

series and other upcoming Nosy Crow books
visit

www.nosycrow.com

To read an extract from

Olivia
and the
Movie Stars

turn the page!

nosy
crow

Chapter One

"It's very odd," said Georgia, who was leaning out of the dance studio window on the second floor of the Swan Academy of Theatre and Dance. "There are two men and a woman with cameras hiding in the bushes down by the front steps. Do you think we should tell Miss Swan?"

"Let me see," said Tom, jumping off the high wire, brushing back his red hair and running over to the window. He gave a little whistle. "Georgia's right. And there's another photographer sitting in that blue BMW across the street. The Swan's being staked out; someone famous must be coming to visit!"

The children were used to famous people visiting the Swan, particularly ex-pupils. *Hot* magazine had recently done an entire photo-feature about the princess of pop, Amber Lavelle, returning to her former school, and at the end of last term, old boy Theo Deacon, who was playing Hamlet at the National Theatre, had come to give a talk to the senior pupils. But there was something different about today. Even as they were watching, a camera crew turned up, and they were swiftly followed by two large men wearing dark suits and sunglasses who looked around shiftily as if they were secret-service agents in a bad American spy movie.

"*He* doesn't look like someone from the press," said Eel, pointing at one of the men. He saw her and scowled, then turned his back and eyed a group of Swan pupils making their way up the front steps of the school, some already wearing their practice clothes with ballet shoes slung around their necks. He watched them closely as if he thought that their leotards and legwarmers were very suspicious and clear evidence of criminal intent.

"Maybe they're just pretending to be photographers and they're really undercover police officers investigating a terrible crime!" said Eel. "That man's moustache looks fake to me; it's exactly like the one you wore in

Bugsy Malone, Tom." She wriggled excitedly at the thought, showing just why she'd got her nickname.

"Why would the police want to stake out a stage school?" asked Ayesha, reasonably.

"For crimes against art?" said Tom with a grin. "Maybe someone reported your performance in the end of term concert to *Crimestoppers*, Eel. You're probably about to be arrested for murdering pirouettes." Eel looked so indignant that everyone laughed.

"Only joking," said Tom hurriedly. "You're a brilliant dancer. The best."

"I'm not quite the best," said Eel. "Not yet, anyway. But one day I will be, if I keep practising." She knew that talent wasn't enough; if she was going to be a great dancer she had to work her socks off, and then she would need some luck, too.

"Well, I think we ought to tell Miss Swan about the photographers," said Georgia.

"She already knows," came a quiet voice. Everyone swung around to look at Olivia Marvell, who was balanced on one foot on the high wire suspended across the dance studio. She was reflected back at them several times in the huge mirrors hung on the walls. Unfazed by her friends' attention, she coolly performed a perfect somersault to dismount. As she untied her long dark hair, a gentle smile twitched around the corners of her mouth and her eyes sparkled, giving her serious face a luminous quality as if it was lit from within.

"Liv Marvell, you've been keeping secrets from your best friends, and you know that's not allowed," said Tom accusingly.

"*And* from your little sister. It's an outrage," said Eel with a jiggle. Olivia looked guilty; she felt really torn. She longed to tell them everything she'd discovered that morning. She'd overheard her grandmother talking on her mobile to the theatre director, Jon James, who had recently had a big hit on the West End stage with a revival of *The Sound of Music*. It was clear from what Olivia had heard that Jon was planning a new production of a very famous play with an all-star Hollywood casting. But she had promised Gran that she wouldn't say a word until Alicia herself had made an announcement at the traditional start of term assembly.

Olivia felt really tempted to spill the beans. After all, everyone would know why the photographers and bodyguards were outside in about half an hour, so did it really matter if she told her friends a few minutes early? It could do no harm, surely. But she didn't want to break Alicia's trust. And anyway, it made her feel quite tingly and powerful to know something that no one else did, and which everyone was desperate to find out about. She thought she'd enjoy the feeling for just a little bit longer…

Look out for more fabulous fiction
from Nosy Crow!

Coming soon...